Lola's Muse

Also by RA Cook

Calvin Splinter & His Splendid Splinter Ideas
GIGANTA, An Epic Tale
Lola's Muse, Limited Edition, 2022
Going Out the IN Road

Lola's Muse

*A Short Story Collection
Filled with Whimsy and Wonder*

Expanded Edition, 2025

R A Cook

HMAPUB
Publisher of Books, Stories & Cards

Disclaimer
The author and publisher shall have neither liability nor
responsibility to any person or entity with respect
to any perceived loss or damage caused, directly or indirectly
by the information contained in this book.

Cover and interior design by RA Cook
Illustrations by RA Cook

Set in Adobe Caslon Pro
Printed in the U.S.A.

Library of Congress Cataloging-in-Publication Data
Rebecca Cook
Lola's Muse
by RA Cook
1. Fiction 2. Magical Realism 3. Short Stories

ISBN: 979-8-9883778-4-9, ebook: 979-8-9883778-5-6
Library of Congress Control Number:
2024923152

Expanded Edition, 2025

HMA Publishing
Publisher of Books, Stories & Cards
www.hmapublishing.com

Table of Contents

Dedicated to

Henry and Leanora

Lola's Muse

1 Amsterdam

After an odd series of events that she couldn't quite remember, Lola found herself lying on a long, wooden bench. She sat up and searched her bag for a compact mirror. Shocked at her appearance, Lola grimaced. Her hair was so matted it looked as if she'd been through a windstorm. After plucking a few stray feathers out of her hair, she brushed back her carrot red tresses and blinked through the dark, haunting eye makeup she'd applied so carefully yesterday. Smeared beyond recognition, the murky mascara made it difficult to see. Where was her new purple hat that she'd proudly worn yesterday? *What happened to that?*

Lola clenched her jaw and concentrated, willing her memory to work, but her mind still felt a bit fuzzy. When she turned her head the slightest degree, she saw double. Objects around her jiggled—even the buildings. She put her mirror back and snapped her purse shut. Thankfully, her green sequined bag was still wrapped around her wrist.

In an effort to force things to stop moving, she grabbed the bench with one hand to steady herself. *Was she experiencing vertigo? Maybe,* she thought. With her other hand, she wiped her face with a crumpled tissue and struggled to remember how she ended up alone, sitting across from the central train station in Copenhagen. She had no clue—no earthly idea how she arrived or why she was here.

"I've come to meet my brother," she heard a voice say. Lola looked around, thinking someone had spoken. "What?" She twisted her body to glance behind to see if anyone was there. "My brother? What's he doing here?" She realized then she was talking to herself—again. This was an annoying new habit she'd acquired since turning fifty.

Moving her head back and forth, she strained to see if anyone had noticed her. She stood and, holding on to the back of the bench for support, she pulled her long, black cashmere coat together. With one hand, she fastened it with the ornamental black frog she'd stitched on last week. She looked down at her scuffed shoes. When she got back to Amsterdam, she'd have to ask Walter if she could borrow his shoe polish. On second thought, maybe he'd buy her a new pair of shoes. Yes, bright red heels—that's what she wanted.

Lola crossed the busy thoroughfare and walked down the avenue littered with shops and wondered how—exactly how—she'd gotten to Copenhagen. *Why didn't she remember?* Crowds of shoppers carrying large packages bustled by on either side of her, but the activity didn't seem to faze Lola. While her mind searched for an answer, Lola meandered along as if surrounded by a protective shell. Despite her dilemma, she stopped to browse amongst the clothes racks outside the fancy boutiques. She couldn't help it. Shopping was what she loved—that and standing alone amongst a throng of people. Being singular in a crowd gave her a sense of privacy. Her aloneness in a hubbub of activity provided anonymity; and yet, she still felt as if she belonged.

Pushing aside several markdown dresses on a spindly clothes rack, Lola thought about her birthday party last year in Amsterdam. Surrounded by old friends, one of them asked her to describe her life so far. She remembered how she put down her champagne glass, held up two manicured fingers, and said with a haughty, uptown intonation, "Two words: exceptionally unusual."

The crowd around the large table had a big laugh, thinking this was a joke—but it was not a joke to Lola. Life so far *had* been exceptionally unusual. She chose those two words for dramatic effect and to create a bubble of mystique.

"Wordplay," she told herself. "That's all it is." Now that she was learning to write she played with words every day, mixed them up like a finely concocted dish, a technique Walter taught her in order to surprise the reader. "Contradict the norm," he coached. Nowadays, contradiction was the norm for Lola. She had been a muse, after all. Hadn't she considered it her sole occupation for years? How many years ago had it been? *How long had she been Walter's muse?*

The first time she saw Walter, she told him her name was Lola, but that was a lie. Lola was not her real name. Her real legal name was Darlene. No one she knew now cared about her real name. How could they? No one knew Darlene—not even Walter. Darlene was that adorable little girl dressed in white, ruffled organdy with black patent leather shoes. Darlene obeyed her mother and father, helped the maid dust, played with her younger brother, went to church on Sunday, and excelled in school—that was Darlene.

She could still hear her mother calling, stretching out the tone of the last syllable for emphasis. "Dar-leeeeene." Even as a young child, Lola couldn't stand hearing that name. By the time she turned twelve years old, she began breaking out of the Darlene mold, experimenting with other names, and demanding surefootedly that her parents call her by the name of her choosing.

After her eighteenth birthday, using a small inheritance from her grandmother, Lola fled to Amsterdam. That's when she changed her name. The very day she arrived in Amsterdam, *Lola* popped out of her mouth in a conversation with a priest on the train ride from the airport. The priest raised his bushy eyebrows in surprise.

"Well, welcome to Amsterdam, Lola," he said in English. His voice was thickly accented, but she clearly heard him say, "May I be of service?"

"Maybe," she said. "I need a place to stay."

"Is that all the luggage you have?" the priest said.

Lola looked down at her overnight bag, a gift from her grandmother. The woven tapestry valise was so full it almost burst when she shoved the heavy bag closer with her foot. "Yes, it's all I have," she said, and blushed.

"How long will you be in Amsterdam?"

"I'm not sure." Lola's voice trembled a little. She looked out the window. The train was making a stop. "I don't have any plans right now. I … I just got here."

"Well, I'm getting off at the next stop. There's a quiet, very nice, little boarding house on the same street as the rectory. I can show you where it is." The priest checked his watch. "They have a lovely café there too. I go there frequently."

Lola smiled. "Yes, that would be helpful," she said. "I don't know where to go and … and I'm getting hungry too."

When they stepped off the train, the priest led Lola down a charming cobblestone street lined with small shops and cafés. The air was scented with freshly baked goods. A cluster of customers ordering croissants and espresso gathered around a pastry shop. Lola marveled at the friendly atmosphere, so different from her life back home. "I like it here," she said and smiled at the priest.

"Yes, this is a lovely boulevard. One of my favorites," he said.

As they walked, Lola's feet wobbled on the irregular stones. She caught her heel between two of the cobblestones, tripped, and grabbed onto the priest's arm. "Careful," he said, and grasped her by the elbow. He held onto Lola for a few minutes until she was steady again. When he let go, the priest gestured further down the avenue to a three-story brick building. "The boarding house is right over there," he said.

Outside the building, wrought-iron tables and chairs, shellacked to a high sheen, were positioned near the café. Bright red potted flowers sat on the tiled steps leading up to the boarding house entrance. When Lola walked through the stained glass double doors into the quaint lobby filled with old world ambience, she knew she was home.

Once Lola settled in her small attic flat, she bought a shiny new bicycle. Attached to the handlebars of her bright red, three-speed bike was a metal basket. The weather was crisp and clear the day she purchased her bike; so feeling buoyant and very grown-up, she pedaled around several city avenues, and then rode along the canal to the flea market.

On a lark she stopped at one booth and picked up a tall, plastic pink flower. Carefully, she wove it into the wire basket and continued on her ride. Cruising along the narrow streets, the flower whipped in the breeze. Lola liked the look of whimsy; it fit her new personality. When she arrived at the boarding house, Lola parked her bicycle in an alcove designated for town bikes. She looked fondly at the flower that marked her new acquisition sequestered in the middle of a sea of bicycles, and then walked into the boarding house. Finally, she felt as if she belonged.

From then on every day Lola rose and by mid-morning set out on her two-wheeler to explore the magic of historic Amsterdam. She rode over arched stone canal bridges, stopped to watch the ships and canal boats and, often midway through her ride, ate a delicious meal at a café—always choosing a different bistro from the day before. Sometimes she cycled over to say hello to her friend, the priest.

"I love it here," she told him one day. "Thank you so much for showing me the boarding house. I've rented my flat for six months."

"How nice for you, Lola. I'm glad I could be of service," the priest said as they walked down an avenue she didn't recognize. "I want to show you a new café that just opened," he said.

"Oh, I wondered where we were going." Lola looked down at her shoes, making sure they were polished. Now that she had forged a new life, she wanted to look her absolute best.

"Yes, I'm meeting another friend, and please join us. My treat." The priest guided Lola around the corner. "It's over there," he said, and pointed to a tall building with a peaked roof and ornate facade. The tapered building looked centuries old and was leaning forward slightly.

"How very odd," Lola said. "I've noticed that some buildings here lean forward like that and look almost like they might collapse. Is there a reason for it?"

"Oh, yes," the priest said. "Hundreds of years ago, the wealthy used that kind of construction so their homes would appear taller and larger. It was a building trick used to enhance the owner's social standing. All in the beholder's eye, let's say." The priest stopped. "Here we are," he said, and ushered Lola into the café.

Just as they entered, a short man in his mid-twenties walked over to them. "Walter, I'd like you to meet my friend. She's just arrived from the United States," the priest said.

❧

That was how Lola met Walter. When Lola told him her name, Walter took her hand and looked into her eyes, as if reaching for her soul—the very pulse that sparked life within her. "Hello, Lola," he said. "*Very* nice to meet you."

Blushing and overwhelmed, Lola blinked for several seconds, trying to muster as much poise as possible. Then she looked into Walter's eyes. "How *do* you do?"

Walter held her gaze. "You have beautiful eyes," he said.

It was at that precise moment Lola felt Walter probe the depths of her inner world. A laser beam of light pierced her protective shell and entered her sacred etheric body. Flustered and unsure of herself, Lola glanced down. "Thank you." She slipped her hand out of Walter's grasp and sat next to the priest.

"Walter, what's good here?" the priest said, and opened the menu. "I haven't eaten yet and I *am* hungry."

As they walked back to Lola's boarding house, the priest warned her about Walter. "He's quick-witted and very smart, but be careful. He goes through women alarmingly fast." The priest looked concerned as they stopped in front of Lola's building. "I wouldn't want you to get hurt. You're so young and free."

"Yes, I am." Lola raised an eyebrow. "He's awfully short, isn't he?"

The priest burst out laughing. "Yes! But that doesn't stop him. He's wily."

Not a week went by before Walter contacted Lola. She knew he'd call and they would see each other again the moment he held her hand and looked into her eyes for the first time. As far as she was concerned, their meeting was meant to be, and she couldn't wait for the challenge.

"What do you do, Walter?" Lola said. More self-assured since their first meeting, she wanted to give Walter the impression she was interested in his *every* word. She also wanted him to think of her as worldly. Lola didn't want him to think she was inexperienced at small talk … or anything else. With her pinky held at just the right angle, Lola sipped her cup of brewed espresso and waited for Walter's reply.

"Why, I work in the arts as a writer and lyrist." Walter puffed out his chest. "I write song lyrics and plays for the theatre." He knew this would impress Lola, and by the look on her face, it did. From the first moment he saw her, Walter sensed Lola's naïveté. Now, as he watched her drink the espresso, he sensed he could easily have her in his grasp. She was ripe with innocence. *It wouldn't take much*, he thought. She was young and malleable. Lola also had something he wanted—something unique—but he'd wait.

"Wow! I've been thinking about becoming a writer," Lola said with schoolgirl exuberance. Forgetting her new sophisticated image, she leaned in toward Walter. "How do you write? I mean, uh, how does it work? The writing, I mean."

Walter laughed and took another drink of espresso, delighted that for at least one minute Lola dropped her staged veneer.

"Oh, my," Lola said, realizing her blunder. To regain her composure, she reached for her napkin and dabbed the corners of her mouth. "Oh, never mind," she sighed and glanced down at her white gloves. Yanking them off, Lola plopped them down on the table. "I'm sure writing is too complicated for the likes of me."

Walter perked up. "Well, it is at times—even for me." With his elbows on the table, he wrapped his hands around his cup. Staring into Lola's eyes, he continued, "Sometimes I write very well." He paused for effect, then peered into his empty cup. "And sometimes not at all. You see, Lola, I wait for the muse and—well, the muse waits for no one." Walter chuckled, thinking Lola understood his meaning, but when he saw the little puzzled twist in her brow, he realized she had not.

"Muse?" Lola cocked her head. Still attempting to reestablish her role as a coquette, she licked her full red lips and pouted her mouth. "What's a *muse?*" she said, exhaling the words in a whisper.

"Why, Lola, someone or something that inspires a person to create, of course, and in my case, write." Walter squirmed in his chair, uneasy with his platitude. He crossed his arms, glanced out the window, and scowled at the passing cyclists.

Lola observed Walter's inner struggle as if from afar. She felt a subtle power shift as if they'd changed roles. She was the teacher now, and he was the student. Surrounded by this sudden feeling of intellectual superiority, she realized he was full of himself like her father. Still, she was captivated.

Just then, Walter's face brightened. "Most writers have a muse," he declared. The metal chair squeaked as he leaned back on two of its legs. Once again filled with confidence, Walter said with authority, "They write songs about it." He clasped his hands behind his head and smiled at Lola.

"Really? Like what?" Giggling, Lola leaned forward. "Name some," she said, challenging him. Their banter, the sparring back and forth, interested her. Lola adjusted her shawl to reveal more cleavage and then folded her arms under her breasts. Nudging her full bosom into more of a cleavage, she waited, knowing she had regained the upper hand.

Walter's face flushed. He cleared his throat so that the timber in his voice deepened. "Why, Homer wrote about muses." Walter put his cup down and sang. "Oh, sing to me, my muse—"

Lola sat back in her chair and laughed. *Poor Walter*, she thought. He couldn't carry a tune; that made her wonder if he could write a song. She put her fingers to her lips to muffle her laughter and continued to listen. Her eyes sparkled.

After ringing out a few more discordant notes, Walter sensed his faux pas and cut his singing short. "Oh, right," he said, and changed tactics. He held up his hands as if conducting an orchestra. "Did you know that in Greek mythology there are *nine* different muses?"

"Nine?" Lola stifled a laugh. "I had no idea—"

"Yes, and, uh—" Walter grabbed his chin and reveled in the moment. "Yes. I believe *Lola* by the Kinks was written about a muse—a transvestite muse."

Lola tried to suppress her amusement, but she just couldn't and burst out laughing. Walter beamed. He had her now.

~

"You inspire me, Lola." Walter took her arm and helped her up the stairs to the street. "You're a muse, Lola. I feel it, and … and I can feel a new song coming right now. Listen." Walter hummed a fragmented melody.

As they ventured down the lane, Lola tried to follow the nonsensical tune, but it was just a jumble of tones to her. When she could no longer tolerate Walter's humming, Lola stopped right in the middle of the crowded cobblestone sidewalk. Touching his lapel, she interrupted him. "Oh, Walter, do you think I'm a muse? Really?"

"Why yes, Lola, I do."

Without another word, Lola opened her purse and searched the contents. She grinned and pulled out a small mirror. "Ah-ha." Pouting her lips, inspecting her teeth, turning her head this way and that, Lola gazed into the compact mirror, preening. After fluffing her hair, she swung her head back with a flourish and laughed. "How flattering! Is this what a real muse looks like?"

"Oh, yes, you're definitely a muse." Walter grinned, charmed by Lola's unabashed vanity. Ebullient, Lola pulled out a tube of lipstick and began applying a fresh coat to her lips. "You're divine, Lola." Walter stared at her. "Absolutely divine. I must tell Priscilla about you."

"Priscilla?" Lola frowned at Walter. Raising an eyebrow, she said, "Who's Priscilla?"

"Why, Priscilla is my fiancé. I … I thought you knew."

"No." Lola stepped back, unable to hide her dismay. "I didn't know you had a *girlfriend*, Walter. Why didn't you tell me? Why I thought—"

"Well, Lola. I'm very sorry if you, uh, I mean, well, if you thought—"

"Yes, Walter. I did think—well, I … I thought you were, uh, romancing me just the tiniest bit. I didn't know there was a *Priscilla*." Lola shook her head; a streak of tears ran down her rouged cheeks. "How foolish of me." Frantic, she searched for a way to escape. "I have to go, Walter. Goodbye," she said, and ran down the block.

"Lola! Wait!" Walter yelled. He did not go after her but watched Lola disappear into the crowd. Then he put his hands in his pockets, turned, and walked to the train station.

~

Lola fled, tears streaming down her face. Once she arrived at her street, she dashed into the rectory to consult with the priest. When she found him in the church vestibule, she pleaded, "Will you sit with me for a few minutes? Please." Lola wiped the smudged mascara from her cheeks and let out a muffled sob. "Walter has a *girlfriend*."

"Yes, dear, I know." The priest held Lola's hands and led her over to a vacant pew. It was midday, and the church was empty. Through the elaborate stained glass windows, the warm sunlight cast a rainbow of colors along the aisle where they sat. Above them, the soft murmur of doves accompanied Lola's weeping, as if joining in with her sorrow. The sound echoed down the long, cavernous hall. "I'm so sorry you're hurt," the priest said, patting her hand.

"Why, why didn't you tell me?" Lola cried. "I feel so ashamed—stupid, really. He flirted with me. I thought he wanted *me* to be his girlfriend."

"Yes, dear, I know. I'm sorry." The priest bowed his head, frowned, and said in a whisper, "I blame myself. I should have explained things better."

2 *Charles*

Charles looked at his Rolex and then glanced out the window. His flight was late taking off from New York, and he was fairly certain his sister wouldn't be at the airport to meet him, especially now that the plane had been delayed. *No, not Darlene,* he thought, running his manicured fingers through his thick, prematurely gray hair. Darlene was never where he wanted her to be. How ludicrous of him to think she would actually *do* something for someone else. She had always been a spoiled, selfish little bitch. *Well, never mind,* he thought. There was plenty of time to figure out how to approach her. The flight over the Atlantic to Copenhagen was long. There were plenty of hours ahead to gestate about how to reason with his sister. Charles leaned back in the comfortable first-class seat, stretched his long legs, and nursed his scotch and soda.

After Darlene ran away from home, Charles remembered feeling secretly glad she was gone—happy even. Finally, he was the only child, a position he'd wanted since he couldn't remember when. There was a five-year age difference separating the siblings, and a power struggle almost always ensued between them. The rift ended, though, when she left, giving him the much desired bearing of a boy king—no longer *the little prince,* as Darlene used to call him.

His victory was partially squelched. The rest of the family had been shocked and traumatized about Darlene's departure, including his grandmother, who had financed his sister's escape with an early inheritance. Remorse and tribulation ricocheted through the household. His mother had cried for weeks. He could still hear her frantic words, demanding that his father find Darlene. "Bring her back," she cried. "Please." With the help of a private detective, his father located his sister, but in the end Darlene refused to come back.

Now, all these years later, he was forced to contact Darlene—or Lola, as she wanted to be called. Charles scoffed at the thought of his big sister's name change. *Lola?* Where'd she dream that one up? How many times had she demanded the family call her by this or that? She had even changed her surname. *What audacity!* Where was her family pride?

Forget about it, he thought. But before the plane landed in Copenhagen, he would have to figure out how to persuade his sister, Lola—a person he did not know—to join the family again. She had an inheritance coming and as executor of his parent's estate, he had to see that she received the money, even if she didn't deserve it.

"Well, hello, Charles," Lola said, smiling at her brother as he walked through the customs gate. "Fancy meeting you here." There was a nervous trill to Lola's voice. It had been a long time since she'd seen her brother. Charles looked older than his age, almost weary. Studying her brother's face, Lola wondered how long it would take before they were at each other's throats again. She cut the thought short, remembering her vow to avoid the eventual argument as long as possible.

"Darlene, you're here. I didn't think you would be." Charles put down his briefcase and held out his hand. "The flight was delayed, I know. I left a message—"

"Lola. *Please* call me Lola, Charles." Looking at her brother's extended hand, she hesitated, then grabbed it with both of hers. His hand felt cool and formal. "I got the message and I'm here." Lola's long, red polished nails touched Charles's crisp French cuffs. She noticed he was wearing her father's gold cuff links. "How was your trip?" she said, pulling away her clammy hands and tucking them into her coat pockets.

"Long as usual," Charles said with disdain. "Do you have a car?"

"No. I, uh, well—" Lola bit her lip. "I thought we'd take the train. Or, if you'd prefer a taxi—" Her brother's brusque manner felt unsettling. Lola wondered why Charles had come all the way to Copenhagen to see her. Couldn't he have just phoned? She was afraid to ask. She didn't want to start a quarrel so soon.

"A taxi would be better, wouldn't it?" Charles peered at his sister. "More direct."

Lola felt Charles pierce through her invisible protective shield she had so carefully constructed this morning. She snapped to attention. "Of course, but you'll have to pay, Charles. I seemed to have misplaced my money," Lola said.

"What happened?" Charles feigned alarm. "Were you robbed, Darlene?"

Lola knew that Charles's remark was uncommonly solicitous for him. Eyeing him, she said, "No, no. I, uh, well, I still have my purse." Lola held up her green sequined bag. "But my money is gone. I … I don't know what happened to it."

Charles stopped short of the curb and searched up and down the boulevard for a taxi. "Shouldn't you call the police?"

"No, I don't think so. There wasn't that much." To avoid more of Charles's courtroom line of questioning, Lola changed the subject. "Are you hungry, Charles? I know a nice little café. We could get a bite to eat, have some tea."

"Well, I could do with a drink about now and maybe a little something to eat. Even in first class, the food is marginal." Like a maestro, Charles waved in a cab and opened the cab door for Lola.

"Charles, dear, I'm a little curious," Lola said after they were seated at the outdoor café. "I'm wondering why you're here. Why did you come all this way to see me?" Lola fidgeted with her fingers and then, pretending indifference, looked out along the promenade. The weekend crowd had established by this time; mingling shoppers strolled by, some fumbling with bulging designer shopping bags. Lola longed to be amongst them. Instead, she braced herself and waited for her brother's bomb to drop. She knew Charles would never have come all this way unless it was important. Unable to stand the pretense a moment longer, Lola whirled her head around and stared at her brother. "What's this all about, Charles?"

"Why, Darlene, er, I mean, Lola, you should be happy I've come. I have some great news!" Charles put his hands on the table and gathered himself as if he were making a public announcement. "You've just received another inheritance—a rather big one this time. Father left you half of his estate, and Mother left half of hers, too."

A large, conspicuous black hole surfaced between the two siblings, as if the air had been sucked out around them. Sitting as if he were made of stone, Charles waited for his announcement to sink in. The gap widened between them as the silence deepened. Then, the scene dissolved and changed as if it were a clip pulled from a movie.

Lola threw down her napkin and frowned. "Oh, that wrecks everything!" she said. Lola knew her brother was angry, but she didn't care. There it was again. Money. Damn that money issue. How dare he bring that up.

Shocked at his sister's unexpected outburst, Charles puffed his cheeks out and exhaled. His face turned red. "What are you talking about?" He stared at his sister in complete dismay. Swiftly combing back his hair with his fingers, he said, "It's a fortune, Darlene. You're rich!" Charles readjusted himself in the chair and tried to stay calm. He picked up the demitasse cup and took a drink. "I can't understand why you're so upset. You can have whatever you want now." Charles sat back, loosened his tie, and crossed his legs. He pulled back the cuff on his sleeve to check his watch.

"Money. Is that all you think about, Charles? Money?" Lola stared at her brother in disgust. "You're just like Father."

"Well, you'd at least have enough for a taxi and a meal, Darlene." Charles grabbed his fork and cut into his pastry. "I can't understand you sometimes. Really, I can't."

"I have enough money, Charles. I do. And the best thing about it is—it's MY money, not theirs."

"What's the difference, Darlene? Money's money, and right now you have A LOT of it coming to you." Charles stabbed at his food and continued to eat. A long span of silence stretched between the two siblings.

Lola picked at her food. "Well, Charles, I guess that's what I'm upset about." She put her fork down and stared down the street. Charles recognized that distant, far-away expression. Darlene had worn it often as a child. For a fleeting moment, Charles felt concern for his sister and wondered if she was well. Lola took a deep breath and exhaled. "All that money might be the ruin of me, Charles. I don't care about money anymore. I want a life. A real life."

"You can still have your life, Darlene. A good one—even with money." Charles's tone was gentle, almost fatherly, but inside he was gobsmacked at his sister's response. *What was she talking about?* She had a cool million dollars coming from the estate—right at her fingertips. *Who wouldn't want that?*

Lola leaned forward and looked Charles straight in the eye. "I want to live the way I want to live and I can't do that with a lot of money. It … it messes things up." She spit the words out at her brother. "I've seen what it does to people." Lola stared at him for a long moment as if he were the devil himself. She started to say something, but changed her mind and rolled her lips taut. She looked down at her hands, and for a few seconds, she toyed with the idea of leaving, then decided against it.

"Have you lost your mind?" Charles sat rigid in the ornate metal chair and glared at his sister. She looked cheap. Her makeup and clothes were gaudy and her bright red hair—what the hell was that about? Sonya, his wife, had been right. Darlene *did* look like a tart. "Look, Darlene, just take the money," he said. A second later, Charles caught himself and inclined toward his sister. In a gentle voice, he said, "Father wanted you to have it. Mother too."

"Well, maybe," Lola said. "I'll think about it." With a concerted effort, she faced her brother. A faint smile crossed her face. "How long are you planning to be here in Copenhagen, Charles?"

"Not long."

"Where are you staying tonight?" Lola opened her purse and took out a tube of lipstick. She smoothed on the glossy red shade without using a mirror, all the while looking at her brother.

"At the Regency," Charles said. "I'm taking a cab. Do you need a ride?"

"Yes, that would be nice, Charles. Thank you." Lola threw the lipstick in her purse and stood up. "I need to go."

3 *An Authentic Muse*

After the short, disastrous first date with Walter, the friendly priest helped Lola reel in her pride. Though she was crestfallen, thinking Walter had deceived her, he had been right about one thing. She was a muse. Deep down, Lola knew it. Spawned by this discovery and knowing her small inheritance would run out, Lola flung herself into becoming an authentic muse.

She began by researching famous muses throughout history and took a particular liking to John Singer Sargent's iconic muse, Parisian socialite, Amelie Gautreau, who sat as *Madame X* in his famous 1884 portrait. There were others too. Manet's *Street Singer* model, Victorine Meurent, and Audrey Munson, known as *Miss Manhattan*, were a few favorites. Lola carefully studied each woman's dressing style and notoriety, then honed those qualities into a unique blend of her own.

Thinking she also needed to be more refined and well-educated, she went on the offensive and bought copious books on every subject she thought might be worldly, and pored over them. She riffled through magazines to learn the latest makeup techniques, and went to fashion shows and high-end dress shops for ideas on wardrobe. She took acting classes and learned two new languages—Dutch and French. Within a year, Lola had conscripted herself into a muselike siren.

~

"What do you think, Father?" Lola said, twirling in front of the priest. She had just purchased a new dress and matching shoes. "Do I look like a genuine muse?"

The priest laughed. "Why Lola, you *do* look like a muse, a beautiful, very lovely muse." The priest took her arm and directed her down the boulevard. "Sophisticated, too, I might add." Lola smiled and nodded triumphantly. "Would you like to have a bite to eat?" the priest asked. "I think we need to celebrate. Don't you?"

"Yes, thank you, Father. That would be nice. Walking confidently on her new heels, she carefully scanned both sides of the street. "I hope we run into Walter," she said. "I want him to see me as I am—a *real* muse."

"Surely you have forgiven him by now, Lola. Haven't you?"

"Yes … yes, I guess I have." Lola blushed. "He hurt my feelings though, Father. But since I'm out in society as a *muse* now, I have a lot of fabulous friends. I know *many* people, and go to *a lot* of parties."

"Then you should thank Walter the next time you see him," the priest said. "After all, without his suggestion, you might not have become a muse, would you?"

"Maybe not, Father, but maybe … just maybe, I knew it all along—" Lola's voice trailed off. She pulled on the priest's arm and halted to admire her reflection in a store's windowpane. "Did I tell you I'm Bastiann's muse now?"

"Bastiann?" the priest said. "I thought you were Stefan's muse?"

"No. That's over." Lola lightly brushed the front of her dress with her gloved hand. "We didn't get along very well. He wanted to rule me and I didn't like that."

"I see." The priest shook his head. As confusing as it was to keep track of Lola and her new life, the priest always enjoyed their visits. Her stories were delightful, and he often secretly thought he might be living vicariously through his young friend. "Here we are," he said, and opened the gilded door of the restaurant. The priest spoke to the maître-d', who then guided them to a table marked *reserved*. "I'll order some champagne," the priest said and waved for the waiter.

Halfway through their meal, Walter walked into the restaurant. Dressed in a fine suit, he stood alone at the entrance as if he were waiting for someone. "There's Walter," the priest said. "Should I invite him over?"

"Well, I don't know," Lola wavered. "Do I look all right?"

"You look lovely, Lola," the priest said. "Shall I?"

"Well, all right. I guess there's no harm in it." Lola shifted in her chair and then smoothed her hair.

"I'll go talk to him. Excuse me." The priest walked over to Walter. As the two men shook hands, Lola took out her cosmetic bag and observed herself in the mirror. She pulled out her lipstick and freshened her lips. Peeking over the mirror, she saw Walter glance at her as the two men spoke. She knew they were talking about her.

"Why, Lola, I'm so happy to see you," Walter said when the men arrived at the table.

"We were just celebrating." The priest sat and pointed to the empty seat next to Lola. "Won't you join us for a bit of champagne?"

"Yes, thank you. Do you mind, Lola?" Walter gestured to the chair. Without waiting for her reply, he sat down. "I was supposed to meet someone here—a client." Walter gave Lola a knowing look. "But the maître-d' just told me he canceled at the last minute." The waiter brought another champagne glass and poured the bubbling liquid for Walter. Picking up his glass, Walter said, "Lola, you look absolutely lovely. What have you been doing to yourself? Uh, I mean, what have you been doing?"

"Oh, I'm very busy, Walter." Lola brushed some crumbs off the table, ignoring the faux pas. "I'm a muse now, you know. Didn't Father tell you?"

"Why, no." Walter regarded Lola and smirked. "A muse, for who? I mean, for whom?"

"Bastiann."

Walter tipped his glass forward, nearly spilling his drink. "Bastiann, the artist?" he said. "I … I thought he was engaged."

"No. Not anymore." Lola leaned toward Walter. "Don't worry, Walter, I won't make that same mistake again."

The blood was rising in Walter's face when the priest cut in, "Well, Walter, what do you think about the new symphony in town? Have you been to any of their recent concerts?"

Walter shifted in his chair. "Uh, yes, Father, I have. Excellent repertoire! A friend of mine plays second cello. We carouse after a concert." Walter stared at Lola. "I'm single again, you know," he drawled.

Lola blotted her mouth with a napkin, uneasy in Walter's penetrating gaze. "Well, I'll let you gentlemen continue on," she said. "I have to meet Bastiann in a few minutes. Please excuse me." Lola skirted herself around Walter's chair. "Thank you so much for the lunch and champagne, Father. It was wonderful." She turned to Walter. "And so nice to see you again."

Walter stood up. "May I walk you to the door?" he said.

"Oh, no, Walter. Don't bother." Lola batted her eyes and rendered a flirtatious smile to Walter.

"Well, it was certainly a pleasure to see you, Lola. I'll be in touch." Walter clicked his heels together and bowed.

4 Sudden Wealth

After Charles dropped Lola off at Walter's suite, she peeled off her clothes one by one, making a long trail to the bathroom. Lola sunk into a steaming bubble bath and leaned back into the antique claw-foot tub. She wiggled her toes in the soapy water. Once again, she was grateful for this small apartment in Copenhagen. It had come in handy for Walter, and now with the recent turn of events, for her too. Lola sighed with resignation. Charles had her. She knew that. The news of her inheritance was the coup de grâce—the fait accompli. Lola hoped Charles wouldn't find out she had lied to him today. Truth be told, she needed money. Still, she didn't want him to know how desperately broke and needy she was. Right now, she depended on Walter, and without his support, she'd be on the street talking to herself just like she was this morning. Somewhere along the line, she'd lost her way. *What happened?*

Soaking in the hot suds, Lola reflected on her past. She stared at the blue and white tiles that lined the bathroom, hoping to pinpoint where she'd turned the wrong corner. Still in a daze, she reached for a towel and stepped out of the tub. Lola wrapped herself snug in a thick, white bath sheet and walked out of the bathroom to the cluttered credenza where Walter kept the bar. She poured a stiff drink of bourbon. "What will it be, Lola?" she said into the silent room.

The strong bourbon tasted sharp, bitter. Lola stared out the window and contemplated her next move. She traced the rooflines and building contours with her eyes, reflecting on the simple elegance of Scandinavian design. She never grew tired of the sparse, clean lines. "Well, Lola," she said, "what are you going to do?"

Then suddenly—bingo! A revelation hit her like a tidal wave. *That's it*, she thought. She had gotten bored with her frivolous life—that's what happened! She had finally, finally achieved total disenchantment as a muse. It had taken quite a while, more than a decade, before the first glint of boredom set in. She should have known then. Lola put down her glass and thought back.

Once she had developed herself into a muselike temptress, Lola flitted around like a stylish, colorful butterfly from artist to musician to writer; round and round from one bed to the next, living off her charisma, good looks and the generosity of her current beau. But after her mentor, the priest, transferred to Hamburg, things changed. Even with all the fluttering around and adulation from lovers, without the priest's friendship, Lola felt lonely. She missed their lunches, their congenial tête-à-têtes, and especially his sound advice and strong foothold in reality.

Out of desperation, unable to span the empty emotional gap left by the priest's departure, she reconnected with Walter, hoping he would help fill the void. It was only later, much later that she realized she'd made a grievous error; her relationship with Walter had been a misfire. She should never have ignored her initial misgivings.

After she gave Walter the nod, he grabbed the reins and took the lead, romancing her and convincing her to live with him. Enthralled by his persistent doting, rarely able to refuse a suitor, Lola acquiesced.

"Let's get married," Walter said one night. They were sitting together, drinking a nightcap on Walter's new Scandinavian divan. "You've always wanted that, haven't you?"

"Married?" Lola turned her head from Walter and rolled her eyes. "Well—"

Ignoring her furtive pause, Walter quickly added, "You know I love you, Lola. I always have." He gently turned Lola's face toward him and looked into her eyes. "Let's do it!"

"Walter, I don't know, it … it seems so, so permanent."

"That's what marriage is, Lola. Permanent. That's why people marry. They want to be together forever." Walter popped up from the divan and walked to the coat rack. He reached into his suit pocket.

"Forever?" Lola tucked her legs underneath her long skirt. "That's the part that scares me, Walter. It seems like such a long time … forever." Lola watched her lover stride over and sit down next to her. "Will you *always* love me?" she said, her voice filled with trepidation.

"Of course!"

"How can I be sure?"

"Here." Walter shoved a small jewelry box toward Lola. "Here's proof!"

She took the velvet-covered box and opened it, then let out a quick gasp when she saw the full carat marquise diamond. "Walter, oh, Walter, it's beautiful!" she said. Her eyes were shining, brimming with tears.

Walter slid on his suit jacket and straightened his tie. With theatric flair, he smiled and plucked the box from Lola. He got down on one knee and pulled out the ring. "Will you marry me, Lola?" he said. "Will you be my one and only muse?"

~

That had been almost twenty years ago. Since then, both Walter and she had fallen in and out of love with each other countless times; each of them claimed an assortment of inconsequential affairs during the marriage. Finally, a year ago, they divorced. To recapture her distant past, Lola moved out lock, stock, and barrel and, with the small alimony stipend from Walter, rented a quaint studio near the old boarding house where she once lived.

Day after day for the first few months, Lola walked the streets feeling empty. Her heart ached. Her sleep patterns broke. She sat up all hours of the night, pining—for what, she did not know. Then, late one night, drenched from night sweats, Lola experienced a life-changing epiphany. As if lightning had struck her, she understood what she was missing, the one thing that couldn't be shoved away or covered with makeup and pretense anymore. In that split second, she felt a powerful surge of insight rise from the deepest, most sacred part of her being—from her core.

For a moment Lola couldn't move, thinking she might explode from the inside out. As if on cue, in slow motion, a vision unfolded in her mind's eye. She saw herself standing in the dark, peering through a tiny hole in a door. Through the miniscule opening, brilliant sunlight shone down on a wondrous landscape. Like a scene from a movie, the illusion panned to a quaint town filled with pristine avenues, shops and theatres, tall spiraling buildings, and luscious parks with sparkling lakes and ponds. Dressed in finery, people milled around open stages, watching actors perform in exotic costumes.

Awestruck, Lola gaped through the hole as the setting continued to fill with flamboyant characters acting out dramatic plays on varying sized wooden platforms that resembled theatric stages. On and on rolled the vignette. Over, around and through the streets, stretching into the distance until she could see no further. At the same time, she was aware that a larger part of her consciousness observed her as she squinted through the peephole.

It was then Lola knew, in a flash, that she'd been blinded. Her life as a muse had been a superficial, theatric sham. All this time, she had fooled herself into believing that acting as a muse was a natural talent, a gift that should be adored. How profoundly silly she'd been.

Yes, Walter gave her the idea all those years ago, and the priest had encouraged her, but it was she, in her youthful zeal, who had grabbed onto the notion with amazing determination. In part, she did it because of money, but truthfully—and this was the biggest part—she craved the attention. She wanted to be special. Without understanding the consequences, she had disregarded her true worth—her own creativity—by offering herself as inspiration to others, most especially to Walter.

There it was, plain as day. She'd used others and had been used too. How shallow her life had been. No wonder she felt so restless, so discontented for so long. She could see now that there was no real satisfaction in fulfilling someone else's dream. She wanted her *own* dream.

Lola felt a gnawing desire to create something that belonged only to her—no strings attached, no patron. It was then the birth of a bigger idea stirred. She could almost feel the cog of a gigantic wheel move inside her.

To celebrate her cognitive breakthrough, Lola decided on a quiet meal at her favorite café just down the block. She wanted to dine alone, to let this huge internal shift sink in without silly, idle conversation. She poured herself another drink. As if by rote, Lola browsed the walk-in closet, handpicking the perfect outfit for the evening. Tonight she wanted to look like a writer—a real one.

Dabbing her face with blush, she contemplated calling Charles. They had to meet soon. He was leaving the next night and if she wanted the inheritance, there was paperwork to sign and a bank account to process. Yes, she would take the money and use it for her dream. As she put on dark eyeliner, Lola thought about the idea that had been kindling within her for decades. It was time to bring it out.

"Hello, Charles?"

"Darlene, uh, er, I mean, Lola. Thank God you called. I was worried that I wouldn't hear from you." Lola heard her brother's concern. "You know I'm leaving tomorrow evening at 5 p.m."

"Yes, Charles. That's why I'm calling. Can we meet tomorrow for breakfast? Say, around 9 a.m.?"

"Certainly, Darlene." Charles sighed with relief. His sister would take the money now. "Uh, I'm sorry. I mean

Lola. It's so difficult for me to call you anything other than Darlene. You realize that, don't you?" Charles paused and then said, "Do you need a lift tomorrow?"

"Yes, Charles, I know. It's okay. Really." Lola tried to keep the exasperation out of her voice. "And yes, I would like you to pick me up."

"Right. Good." Charles moved into his businesslike voice. "I'll be there around 9 a.m. Same apartment?"

"Yes. And, Charles?" Lola hesitated. "Thanks."

The day after Lola signed the inheritance papers, she walked into the bank to check on her new account. The clerk assured Lola the funds were there; Charles had deposited the money as promised. With her account fattened with inheritance, she skipped down the block, almost floating on air, and walked right into a hi-tech store. There, Lola made her first serious acquisition: a top-of-the-line computer. Along with the sleek laptop, she bought a quality printer/scanner/fax machine and paid for a month's worth of private computer lessons.

Not to be outdone by her first purchase, early the next day she whisked into her favorite book and stationery store where she purchased a dictionary, thesaurus, and two reams of copy paper. Jubilant, tossing her flaming red hair back, she marched across the avenue to a high-end furniture store. Walking up to the first salesperson she saw, Lola pointed out the sleek Scandinavian teak desk displayed in the window and bought it on the spot. She added to the purchase a red, high back writing chair with accompanying side table, and to top it all off, with newfound authority, she demanded the merchandise be delivered the very next day. Pronto.

Amused at her willingness to take on something so new, so beyond her capability at age fifty-two, Lola stepped into her new life with vigor. She wanted to be a writer. It was what she'd always wanted. The day she signed the inheritance papers, Charles had laughed at her when she told him what she planned to do with the money. "Darlene, come on now," he said. "What makes you think you can write?"

"What do you mean, Charles? I can write." Offended by his overbearing attitude, she added, "I know how and I have lived with writers for years. Walter, for one."

"Darlene, please," Charles chided. "Don't you think it's a little late in your life for that?"

"Why, no, Charles, I don't." Frowning at her brother, Lola put down the pen he had lent her and crisply stacked the signed papers. Lola snatched her purse from the table. "Are we finished here? I need to go." Arching one eyebrow and boring an icy glare into Charles's chest, she said, "Will you make the deposit tomorrow after you get back?"

"Certainly." Charles placed the pen and legal papers into his leather briefcase and stood up. He grasped Lola's elbow. "Darlene, uh, I mean, Lola, I didn't mean to hurt your feelings. Really." Charles looked down at his feet for a moment and then into his sister's eyes. "I'm sorry," he said. "But surely you see my point."

"It seems you know nothing about me, Charles." Lola pulled her arm away and looked coldly at him. "I know what I want."

Keeping her resentment in tow, she headed for the door. Despite her cool outer demeanor, Lola felt unhinged, ready to collapse. "Goodbye, Charles," she said, and walked out.

5 Franklin

*L*ola knew she wanted to write, but she just didn't know what to write about. For years, Walter tried to encourage her to compose something every day. While they were together, every morning she watched him make entries into a private journal, but she never felt compelled to do it herself. Eventually, just to make Walter happy, she found a pretty fabric covered notebook and jotted down a few words from time to time. Her entries were dated far apart and written somewhat whimsically at first. Later, after the divorce and her life-changing epiphany, she found journaling therapeutic, and as time when on, necessary.

She'd watched Walter work for so many years, so she knew what it took to be a writer. What she didn't know was how much stamina she would need to polish her writing and master the craft, or how agonizingly tedious some days were without a muse. That is, until she met Franklin.

"Didn't I read somewhere recently that all you have to do is *show up, show up, show up?*" Franklin said. He reached for his sleek chartreuse teapot. "Would you like more tea, Lola?"

Franklin, Lola's new neighbor from across the hall, had invited her to tea. It was the first day she'd been out of her apartment for a week. Since Lola had moved to Copenhagen permanently, she'd sequestered in her flat, most days struggling with learning the computer and software, and now with writing.

Last week she'd met Franklin quite by accident. They had both come out of their respective apartments at the same time. Each peeped around their apartment door and tiptoed out as if they were Keystone Cops. It had been such a comedic moment that they burst out laughing and walked down the stairs together, chatting, and introducing themselves.

"I think Isabel Allende said that in a lecture somewhere," Lola said. She felt distracted, and a little disgruntled. She knew this tumultuous feeling meant her subconscious mind churned on a story problem. Not wanting to appear rude, she redoubled her effort to focus on the conversation. "She's an excellent writer. Have you read any of her work?"

"No," Franklin said. "I tend not to gravitate toward female writers. I don't know why." He went over to his bookshelf and, for a few moments, perused the titles. "What do you read? Fiction or nonfiction?"

"Fiction mostly. That's what I write. Fiction. I'm working on a short story now." Lola squirmed in her chair. "I like magazines too. All kinds."

"Have you published yet?"

"No." Lola let out a deep, resigned sigh. "It takes a while to break in, you know, for the work to mature." She walked over to the window and stood for a moment, taking in the panorama. "Your view is unlike mine," she said. "Interesting roofline perspective you have—very different from what I see."

"Hmm. So what about the muse? How long does it take for you to *show up* before the muse steps in?" Franklin smiled as if he'd made a joke. "I'm just curious," he said and fluttered both hands down to his thighs like a dancer.

"Well, that's a tough one for me right now." Lola walked over to the tea tray, picked up a small pastry, and took a bite. "These are delicious. Where did you get them?"

"Oh, just down the street. I'm going there early tomorrow. Would you like me to pick up some for you?"

"That would be nice. Thank you." Lola sipped her tea. "I don't have a muse right now." She licked her fingers. "But I want one." Lola inhaled deeply and held her breath as long as she could. On the exhale, she let out a long sigh. "I used to be a muse myself, you know," she confessed. "A good one too."

"Honestly? How fabulous!" Franklin walked over to Lola. Girlishly, he put a hand on his hip and stood with one leg forward like a mannequin. It was at that moment Lola realized Franklin was gay. She hadn't sensed that before. "Why did you stop being a muse?" he said. He stepped back and shifted his weight.

Lola hesitated. She didn't want to divulge intimate details about her past yet. "Bored," she said and looked at

Franklin with a close eye. "I just got bored with the whole damn thing. It was too much and too little at the same time." She sighed. "After a while, I couldn't see the point of it." Lola sat down, reached for her purse, and pulled out her mirror. "That's when I decided I wanted to write." She searched the contents of her purse, took out some lip gloss and applied the color. After scrolling the tube shut, Lola said with a short laugh, "Now *I* need a muse. That's what I want now." She plopped the lip gloss back into her purse and snapped it shut.

Franklin walked over to Lola and settled next to her. "I'm going to take the train to the Louisiana Museum tomorrow. Would you like to go?" he asked. "There's a new show, some modernists from the U.S. I think you might like it."

"Hmm. Well, it would take my mind off writing. Some days I can't think about anything else. It makes me feel edgy and kind of crazy, especially when I'm using the computer. I haven't conquered that beast yet." Lola sat still and let Franklin's invitation sink in. "Well, I guess I could. I haven't been out lately anyway, and I *do* need to get out." Lola's mood lightened. "What time were you thinking about going?"

"There's a train that leaves at 11 a.m.," Franklin said, "and I've heard there's a very nice café on the grounds. We could have lunch outside if the weather is good. Have you ever been there?"

"Just once, long ago, with Walter. He didn't like it very much, so we left early."

～

Modern, well-equipped bicycle rickshaws pedaled by young, handsome and fit Danish men greeted the train when it pulled into the village that surrounded the famed Louisiana Modern Art Museum. "Isn't this fun?" Lola said. Franklin nodded as the driver helped her into the small two-seat rickshaw. "I forgot about this part. Let's have lunch first and then walk the grounds. I'm starving!"

"Sounds perfect." Franklin winked at the driver as he climbed in. "And it looks like the weather's holding too."

As they moved along the avenue, Franklin noticed his friend was feeling happier by the minute. The dark cloud she'd been carrying around all week had almost dissipated. "I'll pick up a brochure so we can plot our course," he said after they reached the museum. Beaming, Lola waved to him and walked through the museum's double door to check her bag.

The afternoon was a breath of fresh air for Lola. Even though Franklin flirted with all the available, good-looking, young men, he was still good company. She turned a blind eye to his flirtatious behavior. It didn't matter to her, and besides, Lola rationalized, *she had been known to be flirtatious too.* Didn't she once have a slew of her own wiles?

"Oh, the day is so glorious, Franklin. This was a wonderful idea. Thank you." Lola and Franklin sat outside on the grass near a large, voluptuous modern sculpture by Henry Moore. "I love this one, don't you?"

"I do. But, actually, my favorite is the Louise Bourgeois one over there." Franklin pointed to two huge, perfectly round stone spheres. Each charcoal granite orb had a small black nodule sticking out of the center. "I know the sculpture is called *Eyes*, but those look like enormous, round breasts," Franklin teased. "See the nipples?"

"Yes." Lola giggled and blushed.

"You ready to go?" Franklin glanced at his watch. "I think the train will leave soon."

"Oh, I guess." Lola sighed. "It's so nice here." She was having the best time and didn't want it to end. Reluctantly, Lola rose to her knees and stayed there for a few minutes, taking one last look at the grassy field studded with gigantic, modern sculptures. Franklin offered his hand to help her up. That's when she discovered grass stains on her knees. "Oh, dear," she said, brushing at the stains. "Damn, I guess I'll have to go home with green knees. The stains won't come out without soap, I think." She waddled beside Franklin with her hands covering the bright green discoloring. "I have to pick up my bag, Franklin. I'll meet you outside the front door, green knees and all."

Still covering her knees, Lola straddled up to the check-in counter and retrieved her handbag from the attendant. Half of her didn't care about the green splotches. The day had been so grand. She felt light as air, almost giddy. At the last minute, right before she went through the security system, Lola took a quick side trip down a long, glassed passageway. She wanted one last look at an outside sculpture there. The modern art piece had been on her mind all afternoon; she was thinking about using it as a centerpiece in a short story.

Lola checked the film count on her camera and walked through the door to the tiny courtyard where the sculpture sat. There were a few shots left and the light was right.

She focused her lens on the piece and finished the last of her film. Just as she was about to exit, Lola noticed the oddest thing. Off to the side of the courtyard wandered a stray chicken pecking between the cement stones along the pathway.

"What?" she said. "How did you get here?" The chicken stopped, cocked its head, and looked at her. Lola laughed. "Do they know you're here?" The chicken clucked and strutted over to her, bobbing its head. For a moment, they stared at each other. Then the chicken flew up and landed on top of Lola's hat.

Franklin couldn't believe it when he saw the chicken in Lola's large handbag. They were ready to board the train back to Copenhagen. "Oh, my God," he said. "Where did you find that?"

"Shhh, Franklin! I don't want anyone to know I have him, er, her," Lola whispered. "I'm taking it home with me." She opened the bag wide enough for the chicken to poke its head out and smoothed the bird's feathers. Swiveling its plumed head, the chicken looked up at both of them. "Franklin," Lola said, "Meet Henry—or Henrietta, my new muse."

6 Henry

One week to the day after they returned from the museum, Lola rapped on Franklin's apartment door in a panic. "Franklin! Franklin! Franklin!" she yelled in rapid succession.

Startled by the frantic timber in Lola's voice, Franklin snapped shut the novel he had been reading and leaped up from the couch. "Come in, Lola!" he said.

Before he reached the door, it burst open. Lola stumbled over the threshold and into the foyer. Disheveled, she stood hunched over, unable to move. Franklin stared at his friend, unsure what to make of her. She had visibly aged from a week ago. Her weary face was so riddled with worry that she resembled an old woman rather than the spritely person he'd gone to the museum with last week. A chicken feather dangled from her hair. "Lola, are you all right?"

"Oh, Franklin, I have something to tell you—" Lola wrenched off her gloves and twisted the green woven fingers together. Looking down at her hands, she said, "Uh, well … I … well, I've decided."

Franklin hurried over to her. "What about?" He put his arm around her and coaxed her into the living room. "What is it? What has happened?"

"Well, I'm not sure how you'll take this," Lola said, "but please try to understand." Wringing her hands, Lola broke away and walked over to the sofa. She sat down with a thump. "It's just that … uh, well, uh … I'm moving."

"What?" Franklin scooted next to Lola. "Why? What's wrong? We've only just met."

Lola's eyes watered. "Oh, I know, Franklin, but I've got to get a place with a courtyard for, uh, Henry. I think he's a boy, you know." She turned away to avoid Franklin's gaze.

"Oh, that. I thought that might be a problem." Franklin plucked the chicken feather out of her hair and twirled it between his fingers. "I mean, really, how can you take care of a chicken, Lola, for God's sake, in your apartment—three stories up? Good Lord, it must be a mess over there." Franklin flapped his arms and squawked like a chicken. Tickled at his antics, he slapped his knee and laughed. Within a few seconds, Lola bubbled with laughter too. Pretty soon, they were both giggling, their foreheads together.

"I know. It's hilarious, isn't it? A *chicken* living with me!" Lola patted her full bosom, trying to calm down. "And it *is* complicated having one in my apartment. I didn't think about all the fine print when I carried Henry home. Good heavens! My apartment is a mess—smelly too!"

"It's way more than that, Lola." Franklin wiped the tears from his eyes. "It's absolutely, ridiculously funny!" They looked at each other and burst out laughing. Howling, Franklin grabbed a tissue for himself and handed one to Lola.

They were still wiping away tears when Lola stopped. Her demeanor turned serious. "Oh, Franklin, I need your help," she said, and grabbed his hands. "Will you help me?"

"Of course." Franklin leaned into the sofa. He looked down at their hands meshed together and marveled at how his friend could move from one mood to the next so fast. It hit him then that even though they'd been friends for a few months, he was still caught off guard by Lola's abrupt, and often unpredictable, mood swings.

"Oh, good." Relieved, Lola smiled and tightened her grip on Franklin's hands. "I've located a few apartments that might be right for us." Lola blushed. "I mean, for Henry and myself." Lola paused for effect, then with a flirtatious grin, said, "Would you come with me to look at them?"

Without saying a word, Franklin rose from the couch and walked to the side table near the front window. Nervous, he straightened the tea tray and then turned toward Lola. At that moment, he realized he'd grown quite fond of his new friend, and even though she was eccentric—and many times erratic—he loved every minute with her. He couldn't imagine life without her. "Absolutely," Franklin said, "when do you want to go?"

"Right now," Lola whispered. "I've arranged for a taxi. It's waiting outside."

A few days after Franklin helped Lola locate a new apartment, he flew to Greece for a holiday. Meanwhile, Lola packed and unpacked. Anxious for his return, she couldn't wait to see him. The day he arrived home, she called, eager to talk. "Well, it's just what I wanted," she said after giving him a rundown on her progress. "And I know you're going to love what I've done," she said. "Henry has the run of the place now. I had the handyman make a special door so he can come and go, inside and out. You know, like a pet door."

"That's sounds fab-u-lous, Lola." Franklin's voice sounded relaxed, full of sun. "I can't wait to see it." He chortled.

"By the way, how's the writing coming along? Any new pages yet?"

"Oh, not very much. I've only just settled in, Franklin. I picked up writing again a few days ago. It has been too distracting to do anything but move." Lola paused and lowered her voice. "You know, Franklin, I think Henry is going to be a big help. In fact, I know it. He's already roosting on the printer while I write."

"Really? How funny." Franklin grinned at the thought of his friend typing away with a chicken at her side.

"Oh, yes. He watches me type." Lola's voice twittered like a proud mother. "I mean, really, he does! I think he likes the noise the keys make; his head moves back and forth as my fingers hit the keyboard. It's so amusing to watch him watch me. Oh, Franklin," Lola sighed, "Henry is such a comfort."

"Well, who'd da thunk it?" Franklin said, trying to control his mirth. Once again, Lola's bizarre lifestyle captivated him. *A chicken for a muse?*

"I'm busy tomorrow and the next day with some appointments and … and … Walter is back in town too. But after that I'm free. Would you come over Friday for tea?" Lola said. "I want you to see the courtyard. I just bought a cute outside settee for it. Henry would love to see you.

"Yes, Lola, I'd love to. Walter's back, huh? Will he be there as well?"

"Certainly not. We're barely speaking. He called this morning to say he wants to talk to me about something, but he wouldn't say what on the phone," Lola said. "Honestly, that man. What else does he want from me?"

~

Less than an hour after her conversation with Franklin, Lola heard a loud knock at the front door. Wiping her hands, she hurried out of the kitchen, where she had just finished making lunch for herself and Henry. She caught her breath when, through the peephole, she saw Walter standing at the door with hat in hand. "What are you doing here?" she said, opening the door. "I thought you were coming tomorrow."

"Hello, Lola. How's my girl today?" Walter beamed. "May I come in?"

"This is unexpected, Walter." Lola frowned. "But yes, come in. I was just fixing lunch." She stood aside as Walter strode in. "Oh, and Walter, I'm *not* your girl anymore," Lola said. "We *were* married, but we're divorced now. Remember?" Lola shut the door and followed Walter into the front room.

"I know." Walter walked over to the French doors that opened into the courtyard. "But you'll *always* be my girl, Lola. You know that." Walter glanced outside. "Where's the chicken?"

"His name is Henry, Walter, and ... and he's in the courtyard." Lola went into the kitchen and opened the refrigerator. "Would you like something to drink?"

"I'll have a highball." Walter surveyed the room. When he spotted the small bar set up near the dining room table, he rushed over to the antique sideboard. "I'll get it, Lola. You're busy." Making himself at home, he reached for two glasses. "Want one too?" Without waiting for an answer, he started mixing two drinks.

"Well, it's a little early, but I might as well." Lola pulled out a fresh ice tray. "Here's some ice. I was just about ready to have lunch. There's enough for two, Walter. Would you like to join me?" Opening the refrigerator, Lola reached for a small platter of open-faced sandwiches and a relish tray and set them on the dining table. Deciding to feed Henry later, she tiptoed over to the French doors and shut them. Her hand slipped down to close the pet door too.

"Here you go, Lola." Walter handed her a drink and sunk down into one of her posh upholstered chairs. Leaning back into the overstuffed cushions, he sipped his highball. His eyes followed Lola as she set the lunch table. She'd always had such a fine touch with food and dining ambiance. He missed that about her. "How have you been, Lola?" he asked.

"Just fine, Walter. Very busy, you know, with the move and everything." Lola shot a glance at Walter. "I'm *writing* now too."

"Yes, I heard." Walter took a long, appraising glance around the room. From the looks of the fashionable splendor surrounding them, his ex-wife had spent considerable funds on remodeling and the furnishings. "Very charming apartment, Lola. Where'd you get the money for this place?"

"Walter, that's none of your business." Lola spat the words out. She was certain Walter would eventually get around to ask her about the new apartment and the money it took to finance it, but she didn't expect it so soon. Lola doubled her resolve not to tell Walter about her inheritance. She was sure he'd try to finagle some of it out of her.

"Well, I know the scant stipend you get from me doesn't pay for this kind of flat, Lola." Walter chugged down the rest of his whiskey. "What's with the chicken, anyway?"

Lola twirled around to face Walter. Bristling, she put down her drink and walked over to him. "Are we going to fight now, Walter? Because if we are, you can just leave right now."

Taken aback by Lola's unexpected outburst, Walter tempered his voice. "No, Lola, we will not fight. I don't want to fight with you." He set down his glass and took a few cautious steps toward Lola. "I came here to ask you out to dinner. I want to see you again. I miss your company."

"Oh." Lola blushed. "Well, in that case, I suppose so." She sighed. "I mean, yes. Yes, I'd like that, Walter. What's the occasion?"

"Well, I, uh, have something for you. Something I think you'll like." Walter grinned. "Do you want to wait until we dine or shall I give it to you now?" Clowning, he stretched both arms out to the side and wavered back and forth, pretending to walk on a tightrope.

Smiling, Lola crossed her arms and hugged herself. Walter could always make her laugh. Tittering like a young girl, she said, "Oh, Walter, you are still funny. Of course, you know I want it now!"

Walter put his forefinger against his lips. "Shhh," he said. With a swift, magician-like flourish, he withdrew an object out of his jacket pocket and held it behind his back. "Okay. Put out your hand and close your eyes." Excited and a little nervous, Lola teetered in anticipation and did as Walter requested. "Now open your eyes," he said and placed a small jewel box in her hand. "Voila!"

Drawing in a long breath, Lola looked down at the unopened box, and then into Walter's eyes, unsure of his intention.

"Lola, will you marry me?" Walter whispered.

"Again? I mean—"

"Yes, again." Walter put his arms gently around her. He felt her body stiffen in his embrace. "I don't need an answer now, dear, but think about it. I miss you, Lola. I miss *us*."

"But, but … oh, Walter. I don't know." Walter took the jewel case and opened it. In a background of royal blue velvet sat a yellow solitaire diamond ring with a platinum setting. He slipped it on her finger. "It's beautiful. Just lovely," Lola said, her eyes in tears. That was when Walter knew, once again, he'd hit the mark.

7 Walter Again

Enveloped in a coat of dismal gray, the great city of Copenhagen endured another season of dreary fall weather. To avoid the onset of winter doldrums, Franklin spent the chilly afternoon reading. He fell asleep at the end of the first chapter with a book propped up on his chest. As he dozed on the chaise lounge, he heard a faint knocking at his door through the ethers, and vaguely perceived a voice calling his name. "Franklin, Franklin, Franklin." In his sleepy haze, the voice was so distant and indistinct it didn't seem real. Franklin thought he was dreaming until he heard a loud pounding that jerked him out of his drowsy fog. He rubbed his eyes. Wobbling through the study to the foyer, he tried to imagine who was at the door.

Clearing his throat, he said, "Yes. Who is it?"

"Let me in, Franklin! It's me. Lola."

When Franklin opened the heavy, carved mahogany door, Lola charged into the foyer, nearly bowling him over. "What is it? What's the matter, Lola?" Franklin leaned against the door.

"Oh, my God, Franklin! I don't know what to do!" Lola spun around and grabbed onto him.

"What has happened, Lola? What now?" Looking at his friend, he didn't know what to think. She was completely disheveled. The hat he'd bought her sat lopsided on her head. Long, straggly wisps of her carrot red hair hung down limp on either side of her pallid, drawn face.

Smudged with the heavy dark eyeliner she always wore, her puffy eyes looked as though she had been weeping for days.

"I can't do it," she said, pulling off her hat. "I just can't!"

"Wait a minute, Lola, calm down." Franklin took her hands and held them. "Let's go sit. You need a drink. I'll fix both of us one and then you can tell me what you can't do."

"Okay." Shaky, Lola allowed Franklin to guide her into the seating area. She sat down. In a meek voice, she said, "Thank you, Franklin. I really need to talk."

Franklin fixed the drinks and kept his eye on Lola. She looked terrible. Something must be horrendously wrong, but he was afraid to ask again. Right now, she needed a little time to compose herself. She wasn't making sense. "Here you go, dear," he said and handed Lola the drink. "Just take a little swallow. It will do you good." Lola looked up at Franklin and feigned a dainty smile. She took a taste of the bourbon and then pulled out a tissue. "It's Walter," she said and wiped her eyes. "He wants to marry me."

"What? Oh, honey, how awful." Franklin looked at her in disbelief. "I mean … uh … when did this happen?"

"Yesterday, not too long after we talked." Lola blew her nose and then searched Franklin's eyes. "We had sex," she said. "He gave me this ring, and we had lunch, and then … we had sex." Lola held up her hand to show him the ring. Tears flooded her eyes. "I couldn't help myself, Franklin. Honestly, I couldn't."

"Now, now, dear. Take it easy." Franklin didn't know quite what to say. He took a big gulp of his drink. "It's all right," he said, patting her hand. "Having sex is okay, even with an ex. Hell, I've done it before too."

Lola gasped and dried her eyes. "When? With whom?"

"Oh, I don't remember exactly. Jeremy, I think … a few years ago." He waved his hand. "I relapsed, honey, and had a weekend affair with him, or was it another old lover of mine? Oh, it doesn't matter. I ended it after that, totally ended it." Franklin looked into Lola's tearful eyes, hoping his little white lie would help her relax.

When she left Franklin's apartment, Lola took his suggestion and went for a long walk. The best place for that, in her opinion, was the Louisiana Museum. She took the train and headed there. Lola knew Franklin was right; walking around the large grounds would be calming, plus it would be fun to ride in the rickshaw again. She did need to think, and a distraction from all the emotional upheaval would be good.

Lola trusted Franklin like she had the priest. Sometimes she thought he might be the priest incarnate, put in her path again to help her through the rest of her life, as the priest had done long ago. With her thoughts still in turmoil, Lola stepped off the train and headed toward the museum. She planned to spend the rest of the afternoon wandering around the grounds, searching for peace and solace, as Franklin suggested.

"Lola, darling, where have you been? I've been trying to reach you," Walter said. Through the phone line, she thought she heard an inkling of concern in Walter's voice. "I was worried about you."

"Really?" Lola said with disdain. She knew very well that Walter wasn't worried about her, not like Franklin would be. Lola knew Walter was only worried about himself. "I was out, Walter. I had to think."

"Do you still want to dine out … or should we, you know … dine in?"

Lola trembled with indecision. She didn't have to guess at his thinly disguised words. Dine in meant more sex. Right now, she didn't feel like having sex with anyone— especially Walter. She was too confused. "I'm exhausted, Walter. It's been a long day," she said.

"Oh, of course, dear. I'm sorry. I wasn't thinking. I just wanted to be with you again."

"It would be better tomorrow, Walter." Lola could feel Walter's clever nuances creep through the phone line to wear her down, manipulate her again. She hated that part about him.

"Right." There was a crisp edge to Walter's voice. "I'll come by tomorrow around 8 p.m. then. We'll have cocktails and a late dinner, if you know what I mean."

"Fine," Lola said. "And, Walter? Let's go out."

Noma, one of Copenhagen's finest restaurants, was packed when Walter and Lola arrived. Dressed to the nines for the occasion, the two of them created quite a stir as they sashayed through the maze of crowded tables and followed the maître-d' who made sure the couple sat at the best table. Walter slipped him a bill as they sat down. "How's this?" Walter asked and reached across the table to take Lola's hand. He looked at the ring he had given her. "I'm glad you're here, Lola," he said.

"Oh, it's wonderful, Walter. Just fine." Lola let her hand linger in Walter's. She watched him pet her hand as if it were a newborn kitten. She wondered what he liked better, the ring or her hand. "It's lovely, Walter, the ring. Thank you. I'll cherish it."

"Yes, isn't it? I sincerely hope you'll cherish me more than the ring, though, Lola." Walter smiled and released her hand. "Shall I order some champagne?" Before Lola answered, Walter swiveled around in his chair and snapped his fingers. "Waiter!"

The night was mild for the season, so after their robust meal, Walter suggested they stroll back to Lola's apartment. "You don't mind, do you?" He took Lola's hand and squeezed it. "If you're tired, I'll signal a taxi."

"No. It's fine. I'd like to walk. The night is so warm. It almost feels like summer instead of fall."

They strolled along in silence for a while, savoring the autumn air and lively nightlife. Copenhagen, known as the happiest city in the world, was filled with visitors that night. Even at the late hour, the cobblestone streets were bustling with activity. Street vendors still hawked their wares. Walter knew Lola loved to mingle and get lost in the evening crowds, so they stopped from time to time and looked at the merchandise.

This sense of anonymity suited Lola's mood, filled her need to feel elusive. She would never tell that to Walter, though. Walter loved to be noticed; to be the center of a crowd was pabulum to him.

"Have you thought about my proposal, Lola?" Walter said as they entered Lola's flat. "We could get married next week. I'm between plays for a few months. We can honey-moon in Greece … take a nice long vacation. Would you like that?"

"Greece? Franklin just came back from Greece. He had a fabulous time," Lola said, avoiding Walter's question. She wasn't sure if she wanted to get married, let alone go to Greece with Walter.

"Franklin? Who's Franklin?" Walter stopped dead in his tracks. "Are you seeing someone else, Lola?"

"No, Walter. Honestly, stop being so possessive. Franklin is my friend." Lola laughed. "Don't worry, he's gay."

"Oh. Well, good." Walter shrugged, pointing toward the courtyard. "What about that damn chicken, Lola?" Henry was peeking into one of the lower panes of the French doors, bobbing his feathered head and pecking on the glass. "You will have to get rid of that thing before we go to Greece. I can't have it around. What were you thinking anyway?"

Lola froze. "Get rid of Henry? I can't do that, Walter. Henry is my muse. You wouldn't get rid of a muse, would you?"

"If it was a chicken, I would. They're filthy creatures, Lola. How can you stand it?"

"Walter, stop. I don't want you talking about Henry like that. He might hear."

"Who cares, Lola? He's a chicken!" Walter stamped around in a tight circle. He hated insolence. "Get rid of it."

"I can't, Walter. I just can't." It took all Lola had to hold her resolve. Walter nearly always won their arguments, but she wouldn't let that happen this time. Henry was her friend, and he was important to her work.

"Well, you better before we're married. I … I won't have that thing running around."

"Well, you better leave right now, Walter. I don't want to fight and … and I will not get rid of Henry. That's that." Lola walked over to the door and opened it. "Good night, Walter."

"You won't?" Walter stared at her in dismay. "Lola, you're acting strange. All right, I'm leaving." Walter grabbed his coat. "I'll call you tomorrow. Good night," he said and stomped out.

Lola ignored Walter's phone calls for two straight days. Avoiding the phone's frantic ringing unnerved her, but each time she refused to answer, Lola felt vindicated. Each refusal was a minor victory for her—and for Henry. After the third day of rejecting Walter's incessant phone calls, she mustered a large reservoir of inner strength and wrote a letter to him. *The marriage is off,* she wrote, underlining the words twice. Empowered and euphoric after sending the letter, she rewarded herself by meeting Franklin for lunch to tell him the news.

"I've decided not to marry Walter again," Lola said with a determined voice.

Franklin grimaced. He knew his friend was clinging to her recent clarity about Walter, but—. "How is he going to take that?" Franklin said. "Walter seems to me to be very willful and pragmatic. Just be careful." Franklin put his fork down, crossed his arms, and gave Lola a worried look. "With his temperament, I think he could get quite unreasonable if you turn on him now," he warned. "He might go after you or, for that matter, Henry."

"Henry? Do you really think so?" Lola's face turned pale. She appeared ghostlike and limp, as if all will had run out of her. "I hadn't thought about that. He has a key." Lola flailed around, looking for her purse. "Oh, Franklin. What if he knows we're lunching together? We're miles away from my apartment. What if he does something to Henry?" Lola rummaged through her bag and pulled out her apartment key. "I have to go."

Lola ran to the train station. Breathless, she rushed into the car and snatched the last seat. "Oh, my God!" she exclaimed and plopped down. She was sweating profusely. Lola reached for a tissue and began wiping off the perspiration that dripped down her cheeks. She felt the other passengers looking at her. The man next to her smiled politely and then turned away, distancing himself. Lola realized she was creating a scene. She didn't care. This was a crisis. She had to get home.

Walter was out in the courtyard when Lola opened her apartment door. She saw him on the settee, wobbling as he reached upward. "Walter! Stop!" she yelled. "What the hell do you think you're doing?"

"Getting rid of that damn bird, Lola. That's what!" Walter said. "It's got to go!"

"If you so much as touch one feather on him, I'll call the police." Lola hurried into the courtyard and yanked on Walter's pant leg. "I mean it, Walter!" Henry squawked and tried to peck Walter's hand as he held the bird's leg. "Let him go!" Lola grabbed a broom and began batting Walter in the chest.

"Lola, stop! You're hurting me."

"Well, let Henry go and get down from the settee. Right now!"

Walter released his grip on Henry and jumped down. Henry squawked and squawked, then flew higher up the awning and peered down at Walter and Lola.

"Oh, Henry," Lola said. "Are you all right?" The bird looked at her and cocked his head back and forth. The feathers on his topknot flopped wildly back and forth. Lola turned her anger toward Walter and shook her finger. "Get out, Walter!" Lola twisted the diamond ring off her hand and threw it at him. "And take this with you!"

Walter bent down and picked up the ring. He quickly examined it. "I'll call you tomorrow when you've calmed down," he said, and walked stiffly out the door.

"There will be no tomorrow for us, Walter!" Lola slammed the door. Gasping for air, she leaned against the door and listened to Walter's angry footsteps reverberate and echo down the corridor. She stayed there until she was sure Walter was gone.

8 Onward

Autumn fell into winter with a resounding thud on Copenhagen that year. Dark gray clouds hovered around the city as residents braced themselves for the full thrust of November weather. Despite the chilling temperatures, Lola feigned indifference. She bundled up in a thick wool turtleneck sweater, fleece pants, and warm slippers to shield herself from the dank climate. She kept her apartment snug with a cozy fire and always had a hot pot of tea on her writing desk.

Comfortably lost in her writing, she ignored the weather and whittled away on her novel for hours. The first draft was nearly finished. With Henry as her constant companion, she headed to the last few pages feeling a sense of relief, especially now that Walter ceased to call. Finally. The more time and space between them helped the bitterness fade away. As she typed and revised the manuscript, each paragraph, each page, moved her further into a new life.

All of this suited her.

"Thanks for meeting me, Franklin," Lola said. "I so wanted to ride the train again. I've been hibernating this winter, as you know."

"So good to see you too, Lola!" Franklin hugged her. "How long has it been since we've seen each other?" Franklin sat down next to Lola and gave her a small, beautifully wrapped package. "This is for you, dear," he said.

Lola quickly unwrapped the parcel and found an elegant moleskin notebook. "Oh, Franklin, this is just what I need." Lola ran her hand over the smooth tawny leather. "I'm making notes for my next novel now. I can use it for that." Lola gave Franklin a quick peck on the cheek. "Thank you, darling."

Franklin blushed. "I thought you'd like it."

"Yes, yes, I love it!" With a puckish look she said, "I know you have little time today, Franklin, but can you afford me just a small piece of yourself? Please."

Franklin shook his head. "Your invitation is very tempting, but I'm sorry I can't, not today." He gave Lola a sympathetic look and said, "I can't, Lola. I have a meeting up ahead in the next village. Business, you know." He opened his jacket and unwound his wool scarf. "Where are you headed?"

"To the museum, of course. Sure you won't join me?" Lola batted her eyelashes at him.

"Lola, really, I'd love to, but I'll have to take a rain check— or snow check, depending on the season." Franklin laughed and glanced out the train window. The landscape was a blur of white as the train sped toward the next stop. "It's been so wintery lately. I'm thinking about going to Greece again next month. You could meet Alan and me there."

Pretending to pout like a spoiled child, Lola said, "Well, maybe." She lifted her chin and changed her demeanor. "I want to finish my novel before I go anywhere. I'm working on the last chapter now. Let me get back to you on that." Lola took off her hat and twirled it around her hand. "Do you like my new hat?"

"It's quite lovely, Lola." Franklin took the hat and examined it. "I like the shape and especially the color. Purple is definitely you." Stretching the moment out to placate Lola, he turned the hat, inspecting it from different angles. "Very becoming." His fingers moved over the embroidery and tiny sparkling beads as if he were reading brail. "Fine workmanship too." The train slowed. "Well, this is my stop." Franklin handed Lola her hat. "I guess I'll be getting off now."

"When can we see each other again, Franklin? Soon?" Lola put her hat on and stared at her reflection in the window. She meticulously tucked her carrot red hair behind her ears and waited for his answer.

"Of course, darling. We'll see each other soon, especially if you decide to go to Greece." Franklin stood to leave. "I'll call you next week and we can talk about it." He adjusted his coat and woolen scarf and smiled at Lola. He gave her a light kiss on the cheek. "Bye, lovey."

Lola watched Franklin exit the train. Her eyes followed him as he walked down the platform to the elevator. Dear, dear Franklin, she thought. What would I do without him? He's my best friend.

As the train picked up speed, Lola leaned back and listened to the rhythm of the commuter. She closed her eyes and contemplated the last scene of her book. Should she end it with a twist?

⌇

Soon the conductor announced the Louisiana Museum stop. Lola grabbed her large, bulging purse and headed for the exit door. As she got off the train, she patted the squirming bump in her bag. "It's all right, deary," she whispered. "You'll be out soon enough." Lugging the cumbersome satchel, she walked awkwardly down the sidewalk, looking very much like a bag lady. A block before the museum, she stopped, reached into the handbag, and pulled out Henry. Lola petted him for a few minutes to calm him down. Then she put him on top of her hat and stood still while Henry fanned out his feathers. In minutes, he looked like a feathered ornament attached to her hat.

Once Henry nestled in, Lola walked down the boardwalk, carefully balancing him as she went. She knew the two of them were quite a spectacle, but she didn't care. Immersed in plotting the outcome of her book, Lola ignored the strange looks and odd comments from passersby and continued to prattle on to Henry about how she wanted the novel to end. Henry rode along, bobbling his head as if he comprehended every word.

A block past the museum, Lola stopped. Suddenly aware that she had missed the entrance, she stood for a moment looking at the museum buildings behind her, undecided whether to go back. Ahead, she saw a light glimmering on some cobblestone steps that led into what appeared to be a tree tunnel. She had not noticed it before. Shafts of sunlight glinted through the leafless trees as if inviting her into the tunnel. Enticed by the mystical appearance, Lola shrugged her shoulders and, without another thought, continued down the lane.

When she arrived at the bottom of the stone stairs, Lola stood for a moment in awe. Enthralled by the diffused light within the tunnel, she stepped deftly onto the narrow walkway. As she walked along the shimmering corridor, a glow emanating from the trees enveloped her. Bent ever so slightly to form the tunnel, the trees vibrated with extraordinary vitality, as if their trunks and branches were animated beings. Lola felt them reach out and beckon her onward. She could almost hear them talking.

Henry felt the sensation, too, and stretched his neck to crow a loud greeting. His antics made Lola giggle so much that her hat felt like it slipped. She reached up to pet Henry and reposition the hat, all the while continuing to walk.

The deeper she went into the tree tunnel, the more enamored she became. She was aware of her unconscious mind working, churning up another idea to bring forward into her conscious thought. Before too long, she walked into the mist that formed around her. The more she thought, the lighter she became until she rose slightly above the mist, gliding as she went. It was then that a matrix of words and symbols flowed out of her unconscious to her conscious mind and streamed down through her body and into her arms.

To her delight, words spewed out from her fingers and pored into actual sentences, line-by-line, onto the walkway. Lola watched in wonderment as the mysterious script spread out in front of her. "That's it, Henry! I've got it now," she said, and leaned down to read the glowing words.

Tiptoeing along, she called out, "The ending. It's perfect, Henry!" Then, without uttering another sound, surrounded by an orb of gossamer radiance, Lola and Henry vanished into the luminous text.

And then,

He heard a sharp rap on the door and shot up from the divan.

"Franklin? Franklin, are you there?"

Franklin opened the door wide. "Lovey! Where have you been? I was worried."

"Oh, just away, Franklin, to some place, well … different, but I'm back now—at least for a while."

The two friends embraced. When they broke free, Franklin said, "Come in, come in. Tell me all about it." He ushered her into the living area.

Lola took off her hat and fluffed her carrot red hair. "Well, dear, I've been writing again—stories … lots and lots of stories."

Raven Talk

Long, long ago
when the earth was new,
animals thought they were people,
everyone spoke the same language,
and we sang as one.
The raven remembers the words,
even now . . .

—As told by a traditional storyteller

Raven Talk

The sullen gray sky kept me in bed longer than usual. A gloomy, sinking mood hovered around me. Soon despair snugged itself close. To avoid its haunting grip, I grabbed my phone and scrolled through Facebook. That's when I found a short post about the upcoming supermoon: "Don't forget!" the snippet said. "Tonight marks the eve of the supermoon." I sat up. *Oh, boy*, I thought, and dove online for more details. According to the local article, the supermoon would be *exceptionally large* due to the lunar perigee. "At precisely 4:32 a.m. PST, it will be giant," the news report said.

A current of excitement vibrated within me. My body tingled straight down to my toes. In seconds, my imagination took off, flooding my thoughts with dreamlike scenarios. *Maybe they will come*, I thought, and drew in a deep breath. My heart grabbed onto that tendril of hope. Maybe.

The thought of being chosen again lifted my spirits. I felt buoyant, optimistic, and adventurous, so I decided to sleep under the stars that night and pitched my tent in the backyard. Around 11 p.m., I yanked the rain flap off the mesh skylight, crept into the two-man tent and settled in. I searched the black ink sky, eager for a sign—something, anything. Deep down, I knew this was wishful thinking because earlier in the evening I heard the voice say, "Not this time." Again, I shook the thought away and checked my alarm clock.

Twenty years ago, I had experienced a startling event on another night of the supermoon, one that changed my life forever. I didn't know then about such things—or much of anything for that matter. Newly divorced and fresh out of work, I slid into the Pacific Northwest on the hard-won assumption that life would continue, regardless of how broke or emotionally wounded I was. A new job was waiting for me there, and I was excited about the idea of sinking my teeth into something meaty and creatively fulfilling. Little did I know then how my life would play out, but in retrospect, I can say without a doubt, a significant door opened for me that night.

My metamorphosis started a few months after I moved into my studio apartment. The weather was mild that day, so I worked outside pruning trees and a few gnarly hedges. In the distance, I heard a raven cawing—and cawing. The abrasive, incessant sound went on for quite a while. Somewhere along the line, it occurred to me that the raven was communicating to me. So, I took real notice and yelled, "What do you want, for God's sake?"

The raven flew up to a higher branch on another tree. Flapping his wings, he began his incessant cawing again. I frowned at the bird, moved down to the blackberry bushes, and hacked away at the nettles hidden in the thorny hedge. "Be careful," I muttered, knowing if I connected with the nettles sting or prickly blackberry barbs I'd be sorry.

After a few minutes, the raven stopped his noise and flew down to the ground. Out of the corner of my eye, I saw him bobbing his head up and down, browsing the lawn for worms. He moved closer. Eyeing him, I continued working, glad for the quiet. When I lifted the severed blackberry limbs into the wheelbarrow, the raven flew up on the roof of the neighbor's small shed and started to caw again. This time, he looked straight at me as if bent on making a point. *That damn bird*, I thought. *What does he want?* Trudging over to the burn pile, I said, "What is it? I can't understand. You need to be clearer!"

On and on the raven cawed at me, until out of the blue, a voice inside my head said, "He wants you to look at the moon tonight—carefully."

"What? The moon?"

"Yes," the voice said, "look at the moon tonight. It will be full." Then there was silence. The voice and the bird were gone.

I didn't know what to think, so I continued to snip the hedge and mulled over the scene. When I finished, I went into my apartment and tuned the radio to NPR. As luck would have it, the news was on. At the end of the newscast, there was a short story about the upcoming supermoon. Tonight, the lunar perigee would be around 10 p.m.

No problem, I thought. Waiting for the supermoon would be a cinch. Ten o'clock wasn't too late. I checked the refrigerator to make sure I had enough snacks and a few beers. All set. So, I went on with my day. But when evening rolled around, I felt tired. Yard work and a jaunt to the flea market had done me in, and I wondered if I would make it for the lunar event. I trudged to the futon, fluffed the pillows, and set my clock in case I fell asleep.

Shortly before 10 p.m., I awoke abruptly to the sound of loud noises. There was an incredible racket going on outside the living room window. When I pulled aside the curtain and peered outside, the noise stopped. Way up in the big Douglas fir I saw faint silhouettes of birds. Ravens! I counted about twenty of them. By that time, the moon was up, large, and bright. The gigantic orb reflected light down on the lawn and through the dark trees, giving the impression of daylight. I flicked the inside lamp off and stood there staring at the enormous moon. Soon, the birds began to caw and cackle at each other again. This time, it sounded like words—English words.

"Thaddeus, this is *not* a good idea," a raven said.

"Why not?"

"We can't take this human up there. It wouldn't be right."

"Why not?"

"You know why. It's against the credo. Alexander won't hear of it."

"Why not?"

"Stop saying *why not!*"

"Alexander won't care," said Thaddeus. "We can do it. After all, I have *authority* now."

"Authority? What authority? Who gave *you* authority?"

All the ravens started talking at once. From my proximity, I couldn't see what was happening or understand exactly what the rumble was about. I heard the ravens clatter to each other, making babbling, nonsensical, strange sounds.

Then quite clearly, Thaddeus said, "Why, Zion gave *me* authority to talk to all humans. He's over Alexander, you know."

"Ah," gasped the other ravens. "Zion?" they said in unison.

"Yes. It was an honor. I thought you knew."

"No, no, no," chimed the ravens. "We *didn't* know."

"Well, I *thought* you did. Now, let's get down to business." Thaddeus puffed out his chest and adjusted his feathers.

The ravens huddled together around Thaddeus. I was certain they were talking about me, but I couldn't imagine what they were up to. I went outside and tiptoed over to the big Douglas fir. When the ravens saw me, the whole flock lifted off the tree limbs like fighter jets. Following one another, they flew across the expanse of the supermoon. Their silhouetted antics reminded me of a surreal Fellini movie. One raven did a loop-da-loop, another a three-sixty roll while cackling all the way.

Clowns, real clowns, I thought and hurried inside.

I felt restless after tucking in that night—listening to the ravens talk had spooked me. Reading for a while helped, but when I finally did fall asleep, I tossed and turned, my sleep fitful. I woke at 3 a.m. and got up to go to the bathroom, drank some water, and then fell back fast asleep. That's when the dream started. As I faded into the dream, I heard talking in the background and vaguely recognized Thaddeus's voice.

"Okay, she's dreaming now. Are we ready?" Thaddeus asked.

The other ravens clucked their response, "Yes. Yes, we're ready."

"Now, remember, do this calmly and quietly or she'll be afraid. This is supposed to be fun, happy."

"Yeah, yeah, yeah," the ravens said in unison.

"Wait," one raven spoke out. "Where are we going?"

"Oh, for Zion's sake! *Please* do keep up, Matthew," Thaddeus said, his voice gruff. "We're taking the human through our time continuum portal. She wants to know more about creativity. We're taking her *there*, where creativity lies." Thaddeus stretched out his giant wing toward the beaming moon.

"Oh, that's right," Matthew said. "Sorry, I forgot."

"Come now, let's get started." Thaddeus gestured to the robust raven next to him. "Henrietta, you take the lead. Everyone go in slowly. Shhh."

The ravens didn't actually pick me up. They propelled me with the might of their wing power through an opening that manifested out of nowhere. As I went through the orifice, I felt my body turn into a gossamer-like substance. I wasn't in a physical body, although I certainly felt like a body of sorts, light as air, yet with contour. I saw all my appendages and torso. Turning around and around, I marveled at my new form. Then, in an instant, we were off.

We landed in formation on a grassy knoll above a lush valley. Spread out ahead of us was a dazzling green forest. Some distance farther was what truly looked like the Emerald City. Everything sparkled and had a translucent quality that was extraordinary, animated. I saw flickering lights amid far-off spiral towers. Each turret, dressed in brilliantly colored streamers, waved majestically in the warm breeze. To my left, a giant waterfall rippled and splashed down a steep rocky ridge into an enormous deep blue lake. White birds dove and soared above the dark, pristine green tree line. A vibrancy existed everywhere that seemed, to my human eye, unnatural, though instinctively I knew it *was* natural. This was pure essence—as pure as it got. My voice trembled when I said, "Where *are* we?"

"Why, we're coming into the Land of Light and Creativity. At first, it takes some getting used to. I'm Thaddeus, by the way, head of this legion of ravens."

Still awestruck, I whispered, "A … a … pleasure, Th–Thaddeus. You're speaking English. How can that be?"

"We are speaking the *Language of All Beings*. You hear it as English because you are English speaking, but if you were Polish, you'd hear it in that language."

"Oh, I see," I said. Frankly, I didn't see, but knew I had to acquiesce and go with the flow. "Will I learn to speak this *Language of All Beings* as well?"

"Certainly. You have the ability even now. All beings can speak the language." Thaddeus mustered his feathered chest up several notches and stood a few inches taller. I smiled and thought he might even have a swagger to go with that posture.

Instead, I said, "Terr-ific!" Nervous and barely able to contain my excitement, I cleared my throat and monitored my enthusiasm. "Ah, er, what does one do in the Land of Light and Creativity?"

"Why create, of course," Thaddeus said. All the other ravens bobbed their heads and in whispered tones cackled to each other.

"Well, I'd like to visit the city. Is that possible?" I asked.

"Absolutely. We're on our way now." Thaddeus spread his wings. "Stand tall. everyone!"

In less than a nanosecond, we stood at the towering gates of the immense city. Migrating around our little group were all types of fascinating beings entering the city, some on foot while others floated through the gateway. Transfixed by the pageantry, I stood in awe. This was nothing like I'd ever seen—not even in my wildest dreams.

"Are we going in now?" I asked. The strange echo sound of my voice alarmed me. Dumbfounded, I wondered if it had anything to do with the *Language of All Beings*. Was this an effect of the new language?

"Oh, that's just a temporary situation. Don't worry," Thaddeus said. "You should be mellowing out soon. We are at a higher level of consciousness here and it takes a little while to adjust."

I frowned, aghast at Thaddeus. He had read my mind. I gave him a polite smile but made a mental note to be more careful about what I was thinking. I might get caught thinking something untoward, inappropriate. Such thoughts didn't fit in Euphoria—or did they?

"We think many things, hear many thoughts. It is what you do with those vibrations that is important," a voice said. My heart skipped. I recognized the voice and turned, expecting to see someone behind me. But there was no one, only Thaddeus and his legion of ravens.

"Did you hear that voice?" I asked.

Thaddeus cackled. "Let's move into the city, shall we?" he said and took the lead. The other ravens followed in rank. As we walked, the group moved into a lopsided *V* formation with Thaddeus in the front. I was placed in the middle like ballast. We passed through the shining, luxuriously decorated gates and down the middle of a vast lane that twinkled with ambient light from a substance that reminded me of mica. Small flying machines carrying tiny beings glided above us. Exotic winged creatures swerved around my head, while odd looking, chariot-like vehicles filled with nearly transparent, glowing passengers proceeded down the lane.

Matthew walked beside me in the formation. He flapped his wings, leaned over, and said, "How are you doing so far?" I stared at him, unable to speak. When I tried to answer, no words came out. I cleared my throat and tried to form a sound—nothing. I shook my head. "Don't worry," Matthew whispered. "It always happens to humans their first time here." Matthew fluttered his shiny black wings and cawed.

"Settle down, Matthew," Thaddeus said. "You'll scare her." Thaddeus gave me a kind expression. "We're going to the Hall of Light and Creativity. It is there you will learn more about creating."

I nodded and smiled meekly. *Okay,* I thought as we walked into the hall, *I can do this—so far, so good.*

Inside the enormous grandiose hall, we stopped before a vast room in the center, which contained an impressive array of tall drafting tables. Each tabletop had a broad, smooth surface, covered with a luminous shield that resembled a retina computer screen. There were about fifty large tables in the room. Each had one or two beings hovering over the screen. It appeared that some of them worked on artistic projects, using elaborate drawing techniques I did not recognize. Others manipulated unusual *signs,* or used strange, unfamiliar calligraphy skills. From my vantage point, I didn't understand what was happening. I cocked my head at Thaddeus.

"They are creating. This is where all creation starts," Thaddeus boasted. "The creators send out ideas as intuitive thought patterns. When the receiver picks up the signal, the creators then help the receiver to explore further, using the complex transmitters you see here." I started to walk inside the room, but Thaddeus stretched out his wing and stopped me. "We cannot disturb the creators now. Let us go up to the viewing area. You'll be able to see exactly what the creators are working on from there." I dutifully complied. Chagrined, I trudged behind the ravens up a long winding stairway that curved around the circular drafting room. I tried to hide my disappointment but, honestly, I wrestled with my emotions. *Why couldn't we go into the room?*

At the top of the staircase, we stopped near the edge of the viewing area, which encircled the creators' hall. From the bottom floor up to the tall ceiling, the massive room was encased in a clear, soundproof substance that enabled viewers on the viewing level to watch the activity without disturbing the creators' work. The ravens, familiar with the activity below, stood back. I leaned over the balcony as far as possible without touching the clear shield and squinted my eyes for closer inspection. Still unable to see the details on the drafting tables, I let out a frustrated sigh and silently wished I had my glasses.

"Your eyes will focus in a few minutes," Thaddeus said, again reading my mind. "You will have no need for spectacles here. Everyone can see perfectly in this land." I glanced at him, grateful for the reassurance, but I still felt edgy about his ability to read my thoughts. "Oh, everyone can read your thoughts," he chided. "There are no secrets here either." Thaddeus laughed, and the rest of the ravens piped in too. I blushed. Heck, I didn't know. But when I looked down again, I found that my eyesight *had* sharpened. I saw the creators' work in minute detail, and what I saw amazed me.

"Today, some of the creators are working on a weather refinement," Thaddeus said. "They are creating certain cloud and wind patterns that will affect this part of the universe, and hopefully, correct some flaws brought on by human and interplanetary error."

"Really?" I said. "You can do that here?"

"Why, yes, of course." Thaddeus moved toward the balcony. He pointed to several of the tables in the creators' room. "Take a gander at the forms they are creating. Notice the elaborate patterns. Essentially, the formations are part of nature's creation and a type of language that few humans understand today. In all living things, there are certain patterns or structures determined by mathematical equations that reverberate throughout the universe, a geometry of sorts. This is the commonality we all share—the *language* if you will. We have been ordered to bring you here to show you what can be done."

Stunned by this inference, I was unable to respond. *Why me?* I was just a middle-aged, struggling artist in the outback of the Pacific Northwest. I could barely feed myself, let alone be a safe harbor for such vital information. Then I heard the voice again. "You have nothing to be afraid of. You were chosen because of your ability to understand refined, creative concepts."

I was? Who is this voice, and where is it coming from?

Before I could speak, Thaddeus and his legion led me down the stairwell into another room. This one appeared to be a gigantic meeting room. Long, sculpted benches and massive chairs embellished with intricate carvings were situated around the brightly lit, oval-shaped room. Thaddeus invited me to sit in one of the chairs, and then he and his legion stood in formation behind me. In a few minutes, a number of beings streamed into the vast space, some I'd seen in the creators' workroom. *What was going on?* I glanced up at Thaddeus. "Don't worry," he said in a soft, kind voice. "You'll find out soon enough."

As he finished speaking, a strong beam of light came straight down from the domed opening at the top of the ceiling onto a small stage in the center of the room. From the midst of the light came tiny fairy-like beings that reminded me of Tinker Bell. These winged beings swished around the beam of light, moving in and out of it at a quick pace, then flitted around the room as if they were cleaning and shining up the atmosphere. I'd never seen anything like it. Even though there were nearly one hundred beings in the room, no one moved; there was no sound, only an anticipatory silence. I wiggled nervously, unable to settle. I tried to catch my breath. Thaddeus gently put his wing on my shoulder to comfort me and cautioned me, telepathically, to be quiet.

When the tiny, winged creatures finished their cleansing, they encircled the wide beam of light and hovered for a few minutes. Then to my surprise, out of the light beam walked the tallest being I'd ever seen. The entity reminded me of an Egyptian statue, immensely tall and regal. I knew instantly that this spirit had been the voice in my head. I watched in awe as a great expanse of bright light shimmered and emanated from the being and filled the room. I felt touched and enveloped by loving warmth and noticed that the sensation had spread and touched the others too. No one spoke, but I felt everyone communicating, communing with one another. Unspoken thoughts pervaded each of us as we sat spellbound in the warmth of a mother's womb. All at once, I knew each of the beings on a deep, intimate level. It wasn't sexual but it was ecstatic and sensual. Then, it was over.

The next morning, I woke up tucked safely in the middle of my queen-sized bed. I remembered everything that happened but was not sure if any of it was real. Still sleepy, I grabbed my dream notebook and jotted down the details in case I wouldn't remember later.

It's been years since I had that dream. Thaddeus and his legion of ravens have not come back. Nor has the voice spoken to me again, until now. Supermoons have come and gone, and I've spent more than a few wishing I'd get a return trip to the Land of Light and Creativity. So far, that has not happened. Nearing my 65th birthday, I realize the odds are it may not happen.

Snug in my sleeping bag all the years later, I roll over to check the time: 3:30 a.m. From my tent's skylight, I search the ink black sky and see that, indeed, the supermoon is up. The large, glowing sphere is hypnotic. I stare into its core as I wait for my aging, stiff body to awaken. I am aware that my mind has started its ongoing, early morning whirl of creative ideas—often, too many to remember. I relax into the familiar mental swirl and with my mind's eye, watch the matrix flow, over and around, up and through. I try to grab onto a few glints of inspiration—maybe one or two. That's plenty for today. If I'm lucky, one will bloom into three-dimensional reality. Rolling onto my side, I idly wonder if I will ever hear the voice again or return to the Land of Light and Creativity. Just as I let go of the thought, way off in the distance I hear an almost imperceptible voice say, "It's not time yet."

The Tansy Puller

The Tansy Puller

I walked off the ferry wondering how long it had been since I had actually set foot on Orcas Island. "Years," I muttered.

"Huh?" said the guy walking next to me.

"Oh, nothing. Just talking to myself," I said.

"Oh, I do that all the time." He smiled politely. "Just visiting?"

"Hmm, no. Well, yeah, sort of. I've come to bury my sister."

"Oh. Sorry."

"Yeah, me too."

He looked intently at me, and for a brief moment, we made eye contact. "Very sorry for your loss," he said, and then hurried up the ramp.

Ahead, the ferry attendant stopped offloading traffic for all the foot passengers, me included. A throng of us quickly hiked up the steep rampway. I made a sharp right past the Orcas Village Store and walked down another block. Cars bulging with tourists zoomed by as I headed toward the parking lot where a friend left my sister's old truck, Jezebel.

"The keys are in the ignition, as usual," she'd said, and I was reminded then that Orcas was still safe enough for locals to leave their keys in their cars. My sister always did, but that was mainly because the ignition key was stuck and couldn't be removed. I got into the truck, patted the cluttered dash, and started the old girl up.

After making a U-turn in the lot, I shifted into second and cruised onto Killebrew Lake Road, a well-traveled, narrow byway I'd driven countless times through the years. As I moved along, I wasn't surprised to see the same old bumps and potholes. Road maintenance wasn't a huge priority on the island. *But this would be the last time I'd drive on the road*, I thought. *The very last time.*

Cruising down the winding road in quiet repose I reflected on the fullness of my sister's life. Hers was always a world of contrasts: rough, choppy edges juxtaposed with wide swaths of calm water. Not wanting her freedom impinged, she never married. There were the usual breakups and heartaches with the occasional live-in boyfriend, but she managed to laugh heartily after the fact and continued with her eccentric, worldly party. Frolicking in the field with her horses was a favorite pastime. Always passionate about the environment, she planted trees where there were none, volunteered to shore up wetlands, and once hitchhiked alone across the country with her dog. There were no serious medical issues either, well, until the end when all hell broke loose. *Her life had been good*, I thought, *if not remarkable by some folks' standards.*

I slowed to make the sharp turn around Killebrew Lake, aware that the road would soon turn from a paved lane to a crusty, gravel back road. "Yes, I remember this part," I whispered. The tires hit the dirt and spewed sharp gravel behind the old truck.

I also remembered that my sister's voice sounded cranky recently, irritable, as if something hovered over her. Some months ago, she began to complain about feeling winded and stiff, she coughed a lot and said she felt old. We joked about it then. But her death two weeks ago had arrived so suddenly I was dumbfounded and still reeling from the loss. *What happened?* She wasn't that old. Or was she?

"No," I retorted to myself. "Not that old, just tired. Really, really tired."

The road changed again so I pumped the brakes as the truck slithered onto slippery, muddy back road terrain. Decades ago, the Orcas populous had voted not to have this stretch of county road paved, wanting instead to preserve the rain forest; and so, it remains an island dirt road in perpetuity. However, when pelted by seasonal dense rainfall—a weather condition the Pacific Northwest is known for—this section of the road is nearly always slick and precarious.

I slowed Jezebel. Creeping along, I wove the truck around splendid, old-growth trees. Dappled lighting fell onto the slick surface as I eased toward the old barn near

Diamond Lake where my sister used to keep her horses. Off in the distance I imagined her feverishly pulling tansy from the grassy field.

She often lectured me about tansy. "They're poisonous, you know, and invasive," she'd say, grabbing a handful. She pointed to a few yellow and black-striped larvae. "See those striped caterpillars. They're eating the tansy. We want that." Then she'd raise an eyebrow and give me an authoritative look.

Tansy is difficult to eradicate without chemicals. It spreads not only by reseeding itself, but also via underground rhizomes. We both knew that. But my sister was a purist, so I begged off, suggesting she excise the wily weed by spraying. Knowing full well that wouldn't fly, I just nodded and pulled up a few more of the dastardly plants.

Coasting down the hill toward Diamond Lake I remembered the two of us back in the day spending time in that field with the horses running wild and free nearby while we pulled tansy together. Pulling tansy in a ten-acre field seemed a daunting task then and, frankly, still does. But my sister liked anything remotely shrouded in daunting; it was practically her middle name. As I drove along, I thought about all the times, all the moments we shared in that field and how, through thick or thin, we were always there for each other. But now … now I was alone.

"Turn in," a voice said. "Walk over to the field."

On automatic pilot without questioning the voice, I turned into the driveway that led to the old barn. Even though the barn was registered as a historical building, the new owners had not repaired it yet. It stood gray and dilapidated, holding within its walls the memories of cows, horses, and sheep feeding from the long trough that ran through half the building. Now the weathered roof swayed like the back of an old mare. Some of the shingles had blown off over the years. I wondered if the owners would tear it down and then realized that they couldn't; it was, after all, a historical building.

I slid out of the truck, walked around the barn, then squeezed my tired, overweight body through the split rail fence. Still digesting the sorted memories of yesteryear, I gazed down the field toward Diamond Lake.

"Come over here," the voice said.

By now my grief-stricken state was clearing off and I was beginning to feel a little unnerved about the voice. So, I said, "Who are you? What do you want?"

"Go down to the meadow. You'll see."

A bit muddled, I obeyed the voice and numbly walked along the crude logging trail that ran up the knoll. Along the way, I started to hum. I realized it was a tuneless, abstract sound, but the humming seemed to take the edge off. At the top of the knoll, I paused to take a long, expansive view of the meadow and lake below. To my surprise, about halfway down I saw someone—an old woman, bent down weeding. With a start I gasped, my voice caught in my throat. *Oh, my God*, I thought, *it can't be.*

At that moment, the woman looked up and waved, beckoning me to come. I don't know why but I ran helter-skelter down the embankment like the young girl I once was. A big grin formed on my lips as I galloped toward the woman. *How the hell*, I thought, *just how the hell?*

"You've come!" she said. "I hoped you would. Here, help me with this, will you?" She leaned down and pulled some more tansy.

"Sure," I said, as naturally as I could. "How did you get here? I mean … where did you come from? How the hell?"

"Oh, that," she said. "I'm in bardo now. Trying to figure things out."

"Bardo?"

"Yes, you know. Bardo, like the Buddhist bardo."

"Oh." I stood and watched her methodically pull tansy. I tried to puzzle out how I could see my sister if she was dead and in the bardo. I wasn't acquainted with Buddhist teachings then, but clearly she was. Trying to take it all in, I said, "Tell me about it."

"Well, bardo is where the soul goes after the body dies. The Buddhists call this realm of the afterlife *bardo*. It means *in-between place*. And you know what? It is literally in-between. I'm here and not here." She laughed and then bent over and pulled a few more tansy plants.

"I see," I said. "Why are you here and not somewhere else?"

"Oh, I was going to the cottage to meet you and noticed the field was full of tansy, so I thought I'd pull some for old times' sake. You know." She laughed again and flung her long, white hair back over her shoulder.

"How … how do you feel?" I asked. "Are you better?"

"Of course. In bardo you don't have a body, you're just spirit. Well, really not even that if you honor the Buddhist teachings. But we won't go there. Too complicated. For now, let's just talk and pull tansy like we used to. Remember?"

"Sure." I reached down and grabbed a handful of the weeds. Trying to remain calm and act as if talking to my dead sister was normal, I said, "I read somewhere recently that tansy used to be a much admired herb. People used it in tea for parasites. So. it's not all bad."

"Oh, I've heard that, too, but it's still bad for grazing animals. Horses especially."

I stared at my sister pulling tansy as she stretched her once youthful body. I said quietly, "I miss you, you know. I'm alone now and I don't like it."

"It will get better," she said. "Besides, I'm not really gone. I'm just dead."

"How's that?" I chuckled. "I'm having a hard time with this. Really hard. I mean I'm on my way right now to pick up your ashes, for God's sake. That's why I'm on the island. Well, that and to distribute the rest of your things. What do you want to do with them anyway?"

"Just give everything away you don't want. There isn't much left anyway. I gave most of it away last year. Had a great giveaway party, too!"

"Yes, I remember you telling me that." I paused for a few moments, trying to sort things out. My heart was sore, aching but happy at the same time. "Should I sell Jezebel?" I asked.

"Well, I don't know. Maybe donate her to someone. She's not worth much." My sister straightened up, raised her arms high, and yawned. "I don't care what you do with her really. I'm not going to use Jezebel, and you already have a car. So just donate her."

"Okay. I'll ask your friend, Helen, if she knows someone that needs an old beat-up truck."

"Give it to her if she wants it. She has horses."

"Sure, I'll ask her." I paused and then cut to the quick. "What do you want done with your ashes? I was planning to scatter them in the Sound."

"That's a good idea," she said. "I like that idea. Scatter away." She twirled around like a ballerina and then wandered down the meadow a bit. I followed her like a lost puppy. Her body seemed to be wavering in and out as if it was a chiffon scarf wafting in the breeze; parts of her were disappearing and reappearing.

"What should we do now?" I asked.

"Nothing."

A few minutes later, a pair of Trumpeter Swans landed on the lake. We watched them glide down to a perfect landing and swim across the still, smooth water. The sun hit the lake at just the right angle, making everything glisten around the giant birds as they cut through the water.

"I'm going to have to go pretty soon," she said.

"I thought so," I said. "Your body is kind of disappearing. I can barely see your face now."

"I'll be around, though, so don't worry. You're not alone."

"That's comforting, I guess." I bent down and pulled some more tansy. My sister was definitely thinning now. I saw through her to the swans on the other side of the lake.

She turned around and smiled. "Bye for now," she said, and then the rest of her evaporated. In seconds she was completely gone, and I was left at the edge of Diamond Lake, with a handful of tansy, not sure if any of this had happened.

Fairy Hill

Fairy Hill

t's true. I swear it," she said and flung her long white hair back with her left hand. "I've seen them."

"Oh, please ..." I rolled my eyes. *Here we go again*, I thought.

"It's hard to believe, I know, but it's true. I'm sure they live inside that hill." She pointed to a large, grassy knoll across from her property.

I pushed aside the curtain and peeked out the window. The large mound reminded me of the Nordic burial grounds I'd been reading about earlier that day. The contour was similar.

"Over there?" I gestured as she had done. "What do you mean *inside*? When did you see them?"

"Yesterday, in the gloaming. Three of them. They literally came out of the hill, stared at me, and then … and then disappeared behind the tree. It all happened so fast I wasn't sure …"

"So you're not sure."

With furrowed brow she glared at me and said, "I'm definitely sure now. Absolutely. Positively. Sure."

"What makes you so sure now?"

Challenged by my skepticism, she tossed back her long hair again. "Because of the dream I had last night."

I sensed she wanted to be right, so I deferred. "What was your dream about?"

"Do you really want to know or are you mocking me, David?"

"Of course, I want to know, silly. Tell me. Please. I'm curious."

"All right, but let me get another cup of tea." With an air of self-assurance, she walked gracefully over to the kitchen counter and poured hot water into her cup. For years I had watched her use this particular cup for morning tea. It was an elaborately painted mug with stylized cupids and winged angels. She called it her *angel cup*. I watched her gaze into the steaming water until the hot liquid turned dark brown. A few minutes passed before she swirled milk into the tea. It was then I knew she had gathered her thoughts.

"The first time I saw them was last year," she said and walked to the table. "I didn't say anything to you before because I wasn't sure. I thought I was imagining them. But yesterday … yesterday … was different."

"How so?"

She sat across from me and looked into my eyes. "Like I said, I saw them more than once." Then she peered into her cup as if searching for the right words. "The first time, they were up in the maple tree," she said, her voice in a whisper. "You know the one I'm talking about, over there near the hill." She stretched her arm toward the window and pointed to the large knoll about one hundred yards away. "Right back there."

I swiveled in my chair to take a better look. Directly across Thimbleberry Lane, adjacent to the hill, stood a huge, old maple tree. Its textured bark and twisted trunk had weathered many a storm. On this fall day, the tree's yellow leaves were floating down like open parachutes, coloring the ground with a blanket of brilliant gold. "What was your dream about?"

"Ah, yes. The dream." She dunked a wedge of biscotti into the tea and bit off the softened crust. For a few minutes she chewed slowly and gazed out the window as if distracted. "I … I was in a darkened place," she said. Her voice sounded hoarse. "It felt a lot like a tomb. Very deep and cool, but not scary like you'd think." She swallowed hard and turned away. I knew she was searching inside herself to grasp onto her dream. "I wasn't afraid then, you know. The dream seemed so real—serene, actually. I can hardly put it into words now."

I felt intrigued. "Take your time. I want to hear everything."

She blushed a little and went on. "Well, when I opened my eyes in the dream I saw three faces looking down at me. The first thing I noticed was their noses. They were bulbous."

Her face turned crimson. With her foot, she nudged me to follow along. "I didn't know what I was looking at, but when my eyes cleared I saw the rest of their faces. It was their noses I saw first. Large. Round. Very odd-looking. They had big eyes, too. Big noses and big eyes."

"Did they say anything?"

"Not then. It was later when I stood up that they started to communicate and ... "

I broke in. "What did they say?" At once, I realized I'd made a mistake shooting out a question before she finished, but I couldn't help it. I was impatient. If this was real, I wanted evidence, something substantial. "Sorry, that was rude," I said and bit my lip.

Glaring at me, she whispered, "I could barely understand what they said. They talked in such a slow drawl as if they were talking under water. I asked them who they were— why I was there." She raised her head and glanced out the kitchen window as if reliving the moment.

I put down my cup and leaned forward. "For God's sake, what did they say?" Suddenly wanting the old familiar connection we once had, I reached across the table for her hand.

Frowning, she looked down and without touching my hand continued, "It was funny, you know. They didn't say much, only that they wanted me to draw them."

"Draw them?" I slid my arm back under the table.

"Yeah."

"You mean illustrate them? On paper?"

"Yeah."

"What on earth for?" I was taken back. Surely she was mistaken.

"They said they wanted humans to know about them. That it was *time*."

"Time."

"Yes, that's what they said. 'It's time.'"

Sitting back in the chair, I glanced out the window at the maple tree. "Are you going to do that? I mean … it was just a dream after all." I realized how dismissive I sounded, but I couldn't believe she was serious.

"I have to. I promised." She went over to her drawing board and handed me a few pieces of sketch paper. "See, I've already started." Drawn in pencil were several faces with big noses, tall hats, and long, shaggy beards. There were a number of doodles, too, along with a few hand-written notes. Gibberish, really. "Their hats are red," she said.

"Red. Huh … interesting." I turned one of the pages sideways to read her writing. "What do these notes mean?"

She grabbed the pages from me. "Nothing. Just idle thoughts," she said, and stuffed the papers in a folder. "I don't know what I'm doing yet, but I feel compelled to do some formal drawings. Make something out of this, I don't know." She paced back and forth for a few minutes. "I think they need me."

"What about your hand? How can you do that with only one good hand?" A few days ago, she called me in a panic. She had cut into her palm with her sharp Hori Hori garden tool and asked me to take her to the hospital. With tears streaming down her face, she had endured five stitches.

"It'll heal," she said, exuding confidence. "It's much better today. They *worked* on it for me."

"Worked on it? My God." I wasn't sure what she meant so I reached for her hand to take a look at the wound, but she pulled away. Giving me a dark look, she carefully unwrapped her bandage and touched the wound.

"Yes, in the dream they worked on me," she said as she held up her hand. "See. It's better already."

I winced. "What did they do?"

Half-smiling, she stared at her hand. "They sang a song, a healing song. They called it *Baba Nom Nu Yah*." She smiled. "It sounded like this." Then she began to hum a tune, something that sounded monotone, almost tuneless to me. "I think that's how it goes." She continued to hum for a few more minutes. "More of them came in and they gathered around me in a circle, all singing this song." She twirled around and around and around like a dancer, jubilant and youthful as she once was. The lines on her face melted away as she spun.

Abruptly, as if remembering where she was, her mood changed. She dropped into the chair and stared down at her hand. "One of them came into the circle and touched my hand," she said. "I felt all tingly and my hand was very warm. Hot even."

"Hmm." With open palm, I stretched my arm across the table again. She laid her injured hand in mine. We looked at each other, eye to eye, connecting for a long moment. Feeling a twinge of remorse for my doubtfulness, I pulled my gaze down to observe her hand. I had to admit the wound did look considerably better. Still, I was not convinced they had done anything. "What happened then?"

"Then … I woke up." Removing her hand, she walked over to her bedroom door and pointed into the room. "I was neatly tucked into my bed and the pain was gone." She turned toward me. "You can see now why I have to help them. They told me if I did, it would help the world and," she paused, "and … I believe them."

"Well, yes, I guess if it means that much to you, you do need to help them. But, I have to say that I'm personally having a hard time believing in them. Very hard."

"Well, try for goodness sake." She marched over to her drawing table. Picking up two pencils, she examined the lead points. "I need to get to work now. Can we talk about this later?"

"Sure." I slipped on my sandals. "I'll go for a walk. Look around a little." I went over to the door and opened it. "Maybe, I'll see them." I grinned at her.

She didn't look at me. Reaching for her pencil sharpener, she said, "You never know."

I knew she was already into her work, so I walked outside. It was then I saw movement by the maple tree and walked over to inspect the area. Standing at the base of the tree, I scanned the great limbs for any sign of them. *Give me something*, I thought, *anything I can believe in—for her sake, if not for mine.* I stood there looking up for a long time. Just as I was about to leave, I saw something out of the corner of my eye. It was just a flicker, just the barest of movement, but I could have sworn I saw the tip of a bright red hat disappearing behind one of the tree limbs.

High Wire

High Wire

Sir. Sir? How 'bout helping an old vet, sir. Just a dollar. That's all."

"Sorry. Don't have any cash right now."

"Aw, in that three-piece suit? I bet you do." The homeless man squatted on the pavement and grinned. He was missing a few teeth. "Say, man, did you see that guy up there? The one they just rescued. I think they said his name was Joey. Yeah, Joey, that's right."

"What guy?"

"The one who was gonna jump from way up there." The grizzly-looking man stood and pointed with a grimy finger to a high-rise building across the street. "The top of that building right there."

"No. Must have missed it. What was his problem?"

"Shit. I don't know. Crazy, I guess. Reminds me of that French high-wire artist. Remember him? Philippe Petit. I was there that day, saw him sit down on that dang high wire thirteen hundred feet in the air. Balls he had."

"Guess I missed that one too. When was that?" Mr. Three-piece Suit pulled out his wallet.

"Well, you'd have to be about my age to have seen it. In the 70s some time, I think. Don't remember the year. That French guy crossed the World Trade Towers on a tight rope eight times! Yes, sir, he did. *Eight times!* That stunt made him famous."

"Hadn't heard about that." Mr. Three-piece Suit feathered the cash in his wallet. "How much do you need?"

"A dollar is fine, sir, if you have it. Talk on the street is that that schizoid, Joey—the guy who wanted to jump—lost his job, ran out of money, and got evicted. That's why he wanted to end it."

"Too bad."

"Yeah, man. Ya know bad things happen to nice people too. I wasn't always a street person either. Had a wife. Worked for a circus once too. That's how I know Philippe's world-famous. I guess he's still alive. I don't know. I've kinda been out of the performing circuit since my injury. Had a bad fall in the big top one night and they booted me out." He snapped his fingers. "Just like that."

"Sorry to hear that." Mr. Three-piece Suit quickly pulled out a fiver and tossed it. "Here you go."

"Hey, thanks. Take it easy, man, and uh, God bless."

Leave a Message

Leave a Message

*M*arny stared at her cellphone's luminescent screen. This was the fourth time in five days that the word *ANONYMOUS* glared back at her. *Not again*, she thought. *Who the fuck is this?* She pressed voicemail to check the message. The husky voice wasn't familiar, the message bizarre. "That's enough! Stop it!" she said and stabbed the delete button.

She grabbed her jacket, slammed the front door, and bolted the lock. In quick succession, Marny shot a glance down the street both ways. This precautionary measure was a new aspect of her life. Since the messages had started, she felt as if she was being watched by someone. Spooked, she dropped the key into her pocket and rushed down the street to meet Emily. Their meeting prayed on her mind too. It was her turn, and she wasn't sure how her friend would take this one.

~

Bright slits of sunlight cut through the blinds and across the bistro to the two women huddled at a corner table.

After a few minutes, their lively conversation flattened into dull sentences. Emily chewed her nails. Marny searched her purse for lip gloss. They both knew it was time for Marny's confession.

Emily eyed Marny. She always paid close attention to her friend's body language. Today, Marny looked stressed; her posture slumped like an old woman, her face was tinged with gray. "Okay," Emily said. "What gives?"

"Well, before I start, I was wondering why, just why, we are still doing this confession thing? Aren't we too old? I mean we started the game in high school, for God's sake. We're adults now, and you're married. I mean—" Marny tossed her lip gloss into her bag and frowned at her friend.

"I thought you liked our confessional game," Emily said. "We started it when we stopped going to church. Remember? It was your idea. You thought we were smarter than the priests."

"Yeah, true. I did think so then, but … "

"Come on. No fair. It's your turn. I confessed last time. Let's do it once more and then we'll be even. We can shut down the game after today. Okay?"

Marny rapped her fingernails on the side of her cup. "Okay, but this is the last, the *absolute* last time I'll play *Confession*."

Emily smirked. Marny loved absolutes. "Sure," she said and sipped her lukewarm latte.

Staring into her cup, Marny stalled.

Emily cocked her head. "Go on," she said.

Marny gulped down the last of her espresso and straightened her shoulders. "Okay. But let me preface this by saying you don't have to believe me, even if it's true … and it is."

Emily moved in closer and smiled. "Every teeny bit?"

"Yep. Every single morsel." With a slight grin, Marny split open the wooden blinds behind her and squinted out the window. "I've been having these unusual calls lately," she said, and turned to Emily. "It's spooky, really."

"How so? What's unusual about them?"

"Don't rush me. Give me a minute to explain." Marny glared into her empty cup then looked passed past Emily. "This morning was the last one," she said. "But these calls—well, they're messages really—have been happening for days now. Maybe longer. I can't remember when the first one came through. It seems like a long time ago." Marny paused and took in a deep breath. "They always come from an anonymous number—all of them."

"What do the messages say?"

"They're all different and come at random times too, sometimes late at night, sometimes early in the morning. It varies."

Emily patted the table in front of Marny. "I know this is important, Marny. Tell me what the messages say."

"The latest one—the one this morning—said: 'Dial 011. Listen to the message. It's for you.' And like a dummy, I did. I don't know why I called but I'm glad I did. The voice said—and it sounds like the same voice from the message— 'Check the numbers.'"

Emily smoothed away crumbs from the table. "What numbers?"

"Turns out it was about my bank account. The numbers *were* low. Actually, my account was in arrears by about a hundred bucks. I managed to patch it up, by transferring money from savings and begging them to deduct the thirty-five dollar overdraft charge. They said they would only because I'd taken care of the matter within twenty-four hours. Still, thirty-five bucks for an oversight. Do you believe it?"

"I can't believe what you're telling me. That's what I can't believe."

"I knew you'd say that." Marny shook her head.

"What are you going to do now?" Emily swallowed the last of her latte.

"I don't know. Wait, I guess."

"For what? The anonymous caller to call again?"

"Really, Emily. Can't you see I'm in a quandary? I don't know what to do."

"Call the police. That's what I'd do."

"And say what? I have an anonymous caller who leaves messages telling me my bank account is overdrawn."

"Tell them you're scared. Have you kept a log with times and messages? They'll want to know that."

"No. I didn't think about that. I can remember some of it … most of it, I'm sure." Marny rose from her chair. "I have to go to the bathroom. Stay here. There's more."

Ten minutes passed before Marny flopped down into her chair. "The other day, the message told me: 'Go to the C-Street Market and buy chamomile tea.'" Marny coughed and pulled out a tissue. "Excuse me," she said and blew her nose. "Sorry. He told me to talk with the blonde store clerk and 'tell her you are having trouble sleeping. See what she says.'"

"How odd. Did you do it?"

"Yes."

"What happened? What did the clerk do?"

"She gave me a script, like a movie script with specific dialogue passages marked up. She said I needed to read it that night, that it was my part to play."

"Really? What did you say?"

"Well, I was so surprised that I didn't know what to say. The clerk just smiled. Told me a man gave it to her with instructions to give the script only to me. I left not knowing what to say."

"I would definitely call the police. *Right now.* Dial 911."

"No. Listen. The interesting thing is that the script had to do with our meeting today. It contains our dialogue. You and me talking in the script just like we're doing now. We're even using similar words."

"What?"

"Here. Look." Marny pulled out a thick stack of papers from her bag. Coffee stains smudged the top sheet, the edges curled. She handed the bundle to Emily. "Go to the last page. The words stop when I give you the script."

Emily flipped through the pages. When she finished reading the last page she placed the manuscript on the table in front of them. "Fascinating," she said. "How did he know? I mean about us. It's so exacting."

"Creepy, I think. Don't you?"

"Well, yes. But he's got us down, like he invented us, or something—even me."

"How do you know it's a *he*?"

"You said a man dropped the script off to the sales clerk. Besides, no woman would do something like this, would she?"

"Maybe not. I just think it could be anyone. Anyone here. Maybe a team of people, like *Candid Camera* or *Mission Impossible*. Remember those?" Marny motioned around the room and shrugged. "Why not?" she said.

"I suppose." Emily sighed. "Now that I'm involved, I don't know what to do either. We have to notify the authorities, though. At least, I want to."

"I want to wait. See what happens next." Marny gathered the papers and stuck them into her bag. "Let's go."

The women paid the bill and strolled down the street in silence. Marny motioned to Emily. "Let's go over to the church. I want to pray."

Emily raised her eyebrows and shrugged. "Sure." Dutifully, she followed Marny across the street to the Catholic church. "Maybe we should confess too," she added, quickening her step.

"What about?"

"Well, you know … what we did. I mean when we left the church that last Sunday."

"Oh. I don't know. It wasn't *that* bad. Plus, we were just kids then, you know."

"Yes, but even that counts. A sin is a sin." Emily stopped in front of the marble steps of the cathedral. "Hey! Maybe, it's that guy. Maybe it's him!"

"Oh, good grief, Emily. He was old. He'd be dead by now."

The women climbed the stairs and stood in front of the elaborately carved wooden doors. Emily turned toward

Marny. "I'm afraid. I haven't been in a church since we … uh … since we left."

"Are you backing out?"

"I don't know. I feel a little guilty, ya know. Like I need to be forgiven."

"Oh, for heaven's sake. Stop it, Emily. We'll go in and pray. Confess if you want to and then we're done. It's simple. Lie if you have to."

"I can't lie! What's the point of going to confession if you lie about what you've done?"

"Well, you know what I mean. Just don't tell all of it. That's not really lying. Heck, I can't really remember what we did. What did we do, anyway?"

"We stole the old man's cane, Marny! He was blind. You grabbed it and we ran away laughing. Threw the damn thing in a dumpster down the street."

"Oh, Jesus. That's right. What idiots we were. Didn't we steal something else that day too? I seem to remember filching some lipstick from Ben Franklin."

"More than one." Emily sat down on a bench by the door. "See. We need to confess. He's after us. I just know it."

"Don't be silly. The phone calls must be about something else—someone else. If these are connected it's a long shot." Marny cracked open the heavy door. "Let's go in."

"Just a sec," Emily said. "Now I'm not sure I want to go in. I'm scared."

"Of what?"

"You know, lying. I don't think I can do it."

"Emily, come on. It's just a tiny white lie." Marny frowned

and shut the door. "Don't lie if it makes you feel better. Tell the truth, for God's sake."

"Wait. I want to think about it. If the old man is dead, who's writing the script? Who would do that?"

"God! I DO NOT KNOW!" Marny whirled around and smashed her fist against the door. "You're making me crazy, Emily. Stop it!"

"Don't you think we should do some investigating first? I mean, call the police or something? This is harassment. He's harassing us."

Folding her arms, Marny leaned against the door. "I suppose."

"Well, I want to. I'd feel safer with the authorities behind us. I don't want to be looking behind me all the time."

"Good point. What do we say? What's our story?"

The large church door opened a crack. An old grizzled-looking man peeked out. "Excuse me. May I get through?"

Marny slid over to where Emily was seated. The old man nodded to the women and walked out. "Let's go over there," Marny said, pointing to an outside garden alcove nestled along the side of the cathedral.

Side by side, the women walked down the marble steps in silence and moved along a cobblestone pathway to the garden. In the middle stood a water fountain. Several birds fluttered up from the shallow fountain pool when they approached. Emily gestured to Marny. "Let's sit here," she said.

The two women sat close together on a cold metal bench. Bright orange and gold maple leaves fell around them as they sat in the autumn silence. Marny's mood turned complacent. She was ready to relinquish control and let Emily take command.

"Do we still have to make things up, Marny? I mean, we're adults now, aren't we?"

"Hold on," Marny said and reached into her satchel. She pulled out her cell phone. "I have to check my messages."

Emily crossed her arms and tapped her foot. She'd like nothing better than to go home, pick up a good book and read it right now.

"Oh. My. God." Marny slid her phone into her pocket. Her face turned white. "It's him!"

"What? What did he say?"

"He wants us … he want us to—" Marny jumped up and gasped. "I'm hyperventilating! Jesus! I can't breathe!" She rocked back and forth. "Grab my inhaler out of my satchel. Quick!"

Emily snatched Marny's bag and frantically searched the contents. "Here! Here it is!"

Marny shook the inhaler, leaned over and deeply inhaled the medicine, then stood up and held her breath. She signaled for Emily to wait. After about twenty seconds she exhaled, bent over and inhaled the albuterol again. In a few minutes, the color came back into her face. Breathing normally, Marny said, "God, that was awful."

"Maybe we should get some tea. Let's go back to the bistro," Emily said. "It's chilly out here. We can talk about it there."

"Yeah, I could use a safe place right now."

The bistro was crowded when they entered. A group of elderly women sat together drinking tea. Laughing and chatting, they passed around a heaping plate of hot biscuits.

"Boy, that looks good," Marny said as they passed the table.

"Yeah. Let's sit over here." Emily gestured to a quiet settee in the back. "I'll get some tea and biscuits at the counter."

Intent on her phone, Marny didn't look at Emily when she brought over the tea. She motioned to Emily to be quiet, pulled out a notebook and made a few notations. She looked at her scribbled notes for a few minutes. "Thanks," she said and gulped down some tea. "He wants to meet us."

"Wow. So, he *does* exist."

"Apparently."

"Can I hear his voice? I want to know what he sounds like."

"Too late. I erased the message."

"Oh, come on, Marny. Why?"

"I don't know. I just did. His voice sounded gnarly, like a wizened old, lecherous man. I know I shouldn't have deleted it, but I feel creeped out about this whole thing."

"We have to call the police. Give me your phone."

"No, Emily. They'll confiscate my phone. I don't have money for another one right now. I need it."

"You are really making this hard, Marny. I'll replace the phone if they take it away. Call them."

"I'm going to call *him*." Marny punched in the numbers and jabbed at the audio button. The women listened as the phone rang and rang and then clicked off.

"Try again," Emily said. "He has to be there. Leave a message."

Marny pushed the phone to Emily. "I can't. You do it."

"Honestly, Marny, YOU'RE driving ME crazy!" Emily said and hit redial. The phone rang and rang. Again, there was no answer. The phone clicked off before Emily uttered a word. "It's not letting me leave a message. Dammit, now what do we do?" Emily slammed the phone down. The women fell silent.

An old man with a cane hobbled over to their table. "Good afternoon, ladies," he said. Neither of the women moved. "I noticed you at the church a little bit ago. May I join you?"

"Well, we were about to leave," Marny said.

Emily smiled and nodded slightly. "Yes, we're leaving."

With a twinkle in his eye, the old man smiled. "This shouldn't take long." He dragged over a chair and sunk into it with a sigh. Resting his cane against the chair, he reached into a paper bag and pulled out a sheaf of papers. "I have something for you."

Both Marny and Emily gasped when he laid the bundle of papers down. "It's some kind of script," he said. "I found it on the church steps after you left. I think it belongs to one of you."

"How do you know?" Emily said. "I mean, uh, well, er, we don't know you. I mean, uh, I don't."

"Oh, I saw you walk into the bistro from the church park. I was on the other side of the fountain when you left. I went back to the church because I'd left my cane there. That's when I saw this."

Marny reached across the table. "May I see that?"

"Sure. I believe it's yours anyway, isn't it?" The old man nudged the manuscript toward the women.

Marny frowned. "I … I don't know." She leafed through the pages. "What the hell? I … I don't understand. Emily, look at this!"

Emily stared at the old man for a long moment, then turned to Marny. "What is it? I'm not sure I want to—"

Marny cut in, "The *second act*. The header says *Act Two*. Christ! Our names are in there too!" Marny started to cough. She grabbed her bag and searched for her inhaler. She shook the device vigorously, leaned over and inhaled.

The old man rose from the chair and reached for his cane. "Well, ladies, my mission here is over. By the way, my name is Wayne. Wayne Thomas. I live around here and go to church nearly every day. Seems I always have something to pray for or confess about." The old man laughed and waved. "I hope to see you another day." Taking slow, measured steps, he made his way through the busy bistro and out the door.

"What the hell?" Marny's face went pale. She frowned at Emily.

"I'm speechless," Emily said and thumbed through the pages. "What are we going to do now?" She turned to the last page. "It says we meet the mystery writer. There's no name. No author name either."

"Christ. Where? Where does it say that?"

"Right here. See, in the dialogue. It's him." Emily pointed at the bistro door. "I know it."

"Let's get out of here."

"Where should we go, Marny?"

"Let's go back to the church like we planned and make a confession—a *real* confession this time. No lying."

Walking up the cathedral steps was the last thing Marny remembered until she woke up in the emergency room. Emily sat next to her. Tears ran down her face as she looked at her friend.

Marny jerked and struggled to sit up, but the maze of wires restrained her movements. "Take it easy, honey," the nurse said and touched her shoulder. "You had quite a fall."

"Wh … what happened? Where am I?"

"You're in a hospital, Marny, in the emergency ward," Emily said. "You fell and hit your head. You blacked out."

"Where is he? The man? What happened to him?"

"I don't know," Emily said, wiping her eyes. "Everything happened so fast. He knocked into you. That's when you fell. He fell too, I think. Someone picked him up and helped him. Oh, God, I don't remember. I wasn't paying attention to *him*. I was more worried about you. The priest called the EMTs. That's how we got here."

"Lord. What a mess. My head really hurts." Marny touched the gauze bandage taped between her temple and right eye and rubbed her forehead.

"What about you? Are you okay, Emily?"

"Yeah. Just a little scared. I didn't fall. I tried to catch you. I'm sure the old man deliberately bumped into you, Marny. Like he had it planned."

"Was it the same man? The one at the bistro?"

"I think so, but I didn't get a good look at him—I mean, up close. Like I said, everything happened so fast. They want you to stay here for a few hours, Marny, so they can monitor your concussion. They're worried about a blood clot."

"Yeah, okay. I don't feel like going anywhere right now anyway." Marny chortled. "But Jackson needs food. Can you go by and feed him? His kitty box is clean so he should be all right for the night as long as he gets fed."

"Sure."

Marny leaned back and sighed. "This is so bizarre, Emily. What is happening? I don't understand it. Where's my phone?"

"I have it." Emily held up Marny's bag.

"Oh, good. Check my messages, will you?"

"Can't it wait, Marny? I mean, you've had quite a shock."

"I need to know if *he's* called."

"Oh, all right." Emily searched through Marny's bag, found the phone and tapped on the screen. "Looks like the battery needs charging."

"Damn. I don't have a charger with me. Do you?"

"No, but maybe one of the nurses does. I'll ask. Wait here." Emily smiled and winked.

"Yeah, as if I could leave …"

"Here you go, honey. All charged up." The nurse handed Marny her phone. "Your friend left to feed your cat. She said she'd call you."

"Okay. Thanks. How long do I have to stay here?"

"A few more hours. The doctor wants to make sure you're well enough to walk out of here on your own. You fell pretty hard."

"Yeah. I don't remember it."

"Oh, there's someone here to see you. Do you feel like having more visitors?"

"Who is it?"

"The man said his name was Wayne Thomas. Said he knew you."

"Oh, Jesus. I think he's the guy who pushed me. What does he want?"

"Do you want him to come in? We can send him away if you'd like."

"Naw. Send him in. I think it will be okay. Will you come in and check on us, though, just in case?"

"Absolutely. I'll be right outside."

The old man hobbled in and sat across the room from Marny. Resting his cane against the chair, he said, "Well, now, how do you feel? They said you had quite a fall. I came to see if you are all right. I think we collided."

"Yeah, Emily said you tried to hurt me. Is that right?"

"It was an accident. I didn't see you. I'm blind in one eye, you know. War injury. Vietnam."

"What do you want?"

"To apologize, really. I'm very sorry."

"Why did you do it? Push me, that is."

"Like I told you, it was an accident."

"For some reason, I'm having a hard time believing you."

"Well, there is one thing I came to explain." The old man shifted his eyes around the cubicle. "I'd like to tell you a short story that might mean something to you—and your friend. Where is she?"

"Home. What's the story?"

Before the old man spoke, the nurse stuck her head into the room. "Just checking on you. Everything all right?" She walked over to Marny. "Do you need more water?"

"Yes, thanks."

Filling the glass with fresh water, the nurse turned to the old man. "Sir, you have just a few more minutes in here, and then she needs to rest."

"Of course." The old man smiled and raised a hand. "This will take only five minutes. I promise. Then I'll be gone."

After the nurse left, the old man sighed, and with watery eyes, he searched Marny's face. "Since I returned from the war, my life has been so different. War ruins you, you know. All that killing; people dying all around you does something to your soul. I'll never get over it, not really."

"When I got home, my dad was ill. He'd lost his sight while I was away. In one day, he went blind." The old man snapped his fingers. "Said he woke up and couldn't see. The doctors couldn't figure out why he was totally blind either, but he could never see again. Well, until the last. On his deathbed, suddenly his sight returned. I was there. I know he saw *the light*. I saw him open his eyes in amazement and lift off. That was it. He lifted off and was gone."

"Why are you telling me this?"

"Because." The old man paused, looked down at his weathered hands and then at Marny. "Because he's the man whose cane you stole. In the church. Years ago."

Marny gasped. "How … how do you know?"

"He told me. In fact, he described the incident. Dad said other people in the church saw you too. Once I found out about it, I went to the church every Sunday for, well, at least a year hoping to find you. Back then I wanted to punish you and your friend. Is it Emily?"

"Yes. We were just a couple of wild kids, Wayne. We didn't know any better."

"I finally realized that. Dad said he forgave you the day someone bought him a new cane. It was the priest, I think. He saw the whole thing. Knew who you girls were."

"Well, I'm glad he got a new cane. It was a nasty thing to do and I'm sorry. I don't know why I did it. I'm not like that anymore. I wouldn't hurt a fly, or steal anything."

"Of course." The old man pushed himself out of the chair and grabbed his cane. "That's all I wanted you to know— that you were forgiven."

Marny's phone rang. She stretched to reach it, but she was too far away. "Can you hand me the phone, please?"

"Sure." The old man moved slowly. By the time he handed the phone to Marny, it had stopped ringing. "Try to get some rest," he said and headed out the door.

"Marny? Are you home?" Emily said.

"Not yet. In a taxi now, on my way."

"Oh, good. How do you feel? Head still hurt?"

"Yep, but not too bad. They gave me something for it. Oh, I had a guest after you left. Wayne Thomas. He said it was an *accident*. I don't know if I believe him or not, but he did apologize."

"Jesus. What gall."

"There's more." Marny paused. "Wait. I'm getting out of the taxi right now. I'll call you back."

The instant Marny walked into her apartment she felt relief. With a loud, piercing meow, Jackson sauntered down the hallway and skittered over to her. She stroked his svelte back and picked him up. "Boy, Jackson, am I glad to see you!" She buried her head in his silky fur and listened to his thunderous purr. "I'm tired, boy. It's been quite a day."

Suddenly, the phone rang, jarring her sense of peace. Marny put down the cat and reached into her bag, but she was too late. For one long minute, she stared at the digital screen. In all caps, the letters *ANONYMOUS* stared back. Her hand shook when she pressed the message button. She expected to hear his voice, but the only sound was a click on the other end.

White Knight

White Knight

A stark beam of light draped over Jack, Mother, and me as we crowded around my dining table. In the final stages of planning our trip, we scrutinized the road map spread before us. As a couple, Jack and I had planned to drive down the coast of Washington state into Oregon, and eventually, to the Southwest. Since Mother had grown up in the high desert, we invited her on our odyssey.

Overjoyed at the invitation, Mother wanted to share the driving. She leaped in that night and suggested divvying up the road trip into three phases. "Great," Jack said. "Emily and I hoped you'd say that. Which day do you want?" Jack leaned back so she could take a better look at the map.

Mother squinted at the highway routes. Her finger trailed along the map down from Washington to Oregon. "I'll take the first lap," she said. "I love this part of the country." Jack nodded to me, and I marked the map into three travel days, one for each of us. As it happened, there were three climate changes along the way. Fall had set in on the West Coast and the forest drive through Oregon would be radiant with color.

We'd chosen the 101 Coastal Highway for most of our first day. The low, luscious country was picturesque, and above all, safe. Jack and I would be okay with Mother driving that terrain.

I was the only one who had lived in a cold winter climate, so I volunteered to take the high, mountainous road, a more treacherous drive during fall and winter. My shift consisted of driving on a highway that wound through thick forest and steep mountain passes. At that time of the year, there was a possibility of sketchy weather and even snow.

Jack, a recent partner and an amiable traveler, agreed to take the last route: desert land straight to Santa Fe, New Mexico, our final destination.

A few days later, we set out. Exhilarated by the prospect of adventure, we cruised along the sunny coastal highway. I felt carefree and thrilled to be on our way. Little did I know then that my life was about to dramatically change.

Five hours later the terrain gradually altered as we headed toward our designated rest stop where it would be time to switch drivers. But Mother had other plans. I should have known when she tightened her grip on the steering wheel. "It's too soon," she said with grim determination. "We don't need to stop here. I can go a little farther." Before I could protest, we shot past the motel rest stop and soared up the highway headed toward the first mountain range.

Up to now, Mother had handled the van and road well, but as we climbed into mountainous territory, the weather turned. A cold front brought in thick, dark clouds and a chilling, forceful wind.

Ten miles or so later, Mother's energy waned, and she slowed the van. Distracted by the mountain views, her eyes drifted over the deep ravines and steep gullies to the majestic tree lines. Her preoccupation made me squirm. "Mother, we need to get back to our original driving schedule. It's my turn now. You're tired."

"I'm watching the road," she said. After a few minutes, she glanced to her left again and this time swerved. "Oops," she said, and blushed.

Right about then it started to snow. In minutes, the pavement turned slick with sleet. When the van drifted onto an ice patch, I panicked. "Mother, *please* keep on the road."

She frowned at me and corrected the vehicle. "I know how to drive," she retorted. The road and weather continued to worsen. Snow dusted the pavement. Soon a coat of white covered the surrounding countryside. My heart skipped when Mother swerved, and the van skidded on the highway. Frantic, I looked at Jack. He shook his head and bit his lip.

I pulled out the map and rumpled the paper. "Here." I pointed. "The map says there's a small village ahead. Mother, please, let's stop and gas up. It's my turn anyway."

"Fine." Mother leaned closer to the windshield. Big flakes of snow hit the van and covered the road. She flipped on the windshield wipers. "Where did all this snow come from?"

When we pulled into the gas station, there was not a car, truck, or person in sight. The state of Oregon prohibited customers from pumping their own gas, so we sat in the van and waited. Soon a tall, rugged-looking man about thirty-five hurried out of the station. Dressed for cold weather with a sheepskin hat and coat, he smacked his heavy gloves together a few times and came over to the driver's side. "Sorry. I was on the phone." He grinned. "Road crew up ahead stalled. What can I do for 'ya?"

Mother nodded to me. I leaned over her and smiled. "Fill it up, please. Where are the restrooms?"

"Sure thing." He tugged on the hose and pulled it across to the gas tank. "Johns are around back," he yelled. "The keys are hanging on the hook inside the station. Help yourself."

"Thanks."

"You want unleaded?"

"Yes."

The restroom smelled of Pine Sol and sparkled as if it had been freshly scrubbed. A full roll of toilet paper and paper towels appointed the tiny bathroom and offset the cracked, stained mirror over the sink. *At least it's clean*, I thought.

On the way out of the restroom, I toyed with the idea of riding out of the station on my mountain bike in the snow rather than putting up with mother's driving. If she wasn't driving, she'd be telling us how to drive. *Poor Jack*, I thought, *he's in for it*.

The attendant still wore his heavy jacket and sheepskin hat when I entered the station. The hat's large ear flaps dangled on either side of his angular face. "Will that be all?" he said. His ice blue eyes stared right through me. He seemed incredibly familiar, as if we'd met before on a more intimate level.

"I think so." I blushed when I handed him the credit card.

"Where you headed?"

"New Mexico. We're taking the long route."

"Yeah, real long." He stared at the name on my credit card. "Emily Johnson," he said. "Nice to meet 'cha, Emily." He looked me in the eye and smiled, then ran the card through an ancient-looking credit card machine.

"Boy, I haven't seen one of those in years."

He nodded. "Yep. Up here we don't have Wi-Fi. Heck, I don't even have a computer. Still have dial tone." He pointed to his old rotary phone. "Funny, huh?"

I laughed. "I didn't think those worked anymore."

"That one does." He handed me the card. "Here you go, Emily Johnson. You be careful now. Storm's a-comin'."

I jumped into the empty driver's seat and waited for Mother and Jack. The attendant had scraped the windshields and brushed snow off the front of the van. I checked my bike. Still there. Mother would have to sit in the rear seat next to it.

Jack hopped into the front passenger side and sighed. "Thank God you're driving now."

"Yep. Weather looks a bit rough, but we'll be out of this pass soon and find a motel. Here comes Mother now. You cold?"

"Emily, turn the heat up," Mother said and slid the side door closed. "It's chilly and this bike—you should have left it in Seattle. Why did you bring it anyway?"

"The heat's on, Mom. Is your seat belt fastened?" I released the emergency brake and drove out of the station with a high degree of caution. Big, fluffy snowflakes dropped on the road ahead. I switched on the headlights. We crawled along the highway. About a mile down the road, the visibility turned into a whiteout. "I'll take it slow for a while until we get through this," I said, and dimmed my headlights. That was the last thing I remember until I woke up in the hospital, my head heavily bandaged, and one leg in traction.

~

Groggy and blurry-eyed, I tried to move, but pain shot through me. I groaned and turned my head to the side. That was when I saw him.

"Where am I?"

"You're in a hospital. You've been in a bad accident, but you'll be okay."

"Who are you?"

"Philip. Philip Estes. I'm the gas station attendant. Also, the ambulance driver and EMT who pulled you out of the wreck."

"Mother? Jack? Where are they?

He paused and looked away. "I'm sorry. They're gone. They didn't survive the crash."

I stared at him. "What?" My mouth went dry. "What are you saying?"

"You're going to make it, though. Doc said I got you to the hospital in time. You had a concussion. Your head hit the steering wheel. We had to pry you out of the driver's seat. Your friend went through the windshield."

"Mother?"

"They think she had a heart attack. She died at the scene. I'm so sorry."

"Yes. Oh, my God, how did it happen? I … I don't remember."

"A semi-truck with a full load side-swiped you. Your van rolled down a steep embankment. The truck driver phoned 911 right away. An EMT nurse and I came in less than five minutes. That's why you're still alive."

"I'm not sure I want to be." Tears streamed down my face. "Poor Jack, and Mother."

"I called your brother. He's on his way."

"Where are the bodies?"

"In the morgue. Your brother will take care of the details. He notified Jack's next of kin. They're coming too."

"Jesus."

Philip leaned in close to me. "I'm glad you made it, that you're alive, Emily Johnson. There's hope in that, you know."

"I guess." I buckled and couldn't stop my tears.

"I'll be leaving now," he said. "I just wanted to be sure you'd be all right." He pulled out a business card. "Here. If you want to talk, you can reach me at this number, rotary and all."

I closed my eyes and whispered, "Thanks."

Grief is a funny, strange bedfellow. It creeps up on you in waves, rolling and twisting your emotions until you think you can't stand it any longer. When the emotional gush subsides, you think you can handle the emptiness, but then another wave of sorrow reaches up and crushes you. I didn't realize how much the loss of Jack and my mother affected me until six months later.

By then my physical wounds had healed. Still, I barely recognized myself in the mirror, but my gaunt, pale face told the story. The small scar on my forehead would always be there as a reminder of that terrible day. I bought some concealer for the red mark and the new worry wrinkles, but I knew the makeup wouldn't cure my misery. I had to do something more pronounced to make the pain go away.

So, at the six-month mark, I decided to make a move, do something—free my aching self somehow. "Take action," I mumbled over and over to myself as I stuffed my makeup kit into an overnight bag. I turned the ignition key in my new car the insurance settlement had afforded me and headed toward Philip. A strong feeling urged me to find him. Maybe he could help me, ground me in some way. I don't know why I wanted to reach out and touch him, but I was compelled, intoxicated with the feeling that he had saved my life once. Maybe he would again. I pressed on the accelerator and entered the freeway toward the high roads of Oregon.

During the trip, I kept Philip's shining, ice blue eyes in my mind. As the miles sped by, I rehearsed what I'd say to him, what I'd tell him—why I'd come. When I signaled to pull into the station, I saw him standing at the center pump helping a customer. I froze. All my good intentions evaporated in an instant. Barely breathing, I stopped the car just short of the other pump.

When he finished with the customer's gas, Philip skipped over, acting like he expected to see me. "Hey," he said.

"I thought I'd find you here." I grinned. "The station looks brand new."

"Yeah. The owner just finished refurbishing the place. It needed a facelift. We've even got Wi-Fi." Philip cocked his head and gave me a half-smile. "Good to see you. How have you been?"

"Okay." My voice sounded weak. "I came to thank you."

"Oh? What for?"

"For saving my life."

Philip bowed, leaned in, and looked deeply into my eyes. "My pleasure, Emily Johnson," he said. "It's my job, you know, or one of them."

"You shaved."

He rubbed his bare chin and grinned. "I was expecting you."

"Really?"

"Well, maybe not today but I knew I'd see you again … someday. You need gas?"

"Yeah. Fill 'er up."

"Unleaded?"

"Yes. I'll pull up." I blushed when he winked.

A silver sedan drove into the station before we said anything more. I watched Philip chat with the young customer, pump gas, and clean the windshield. I wanted to have a conversation with him, too, so to kill time I went to the restroom.

When I closed the bathroom door, memories from the past hit me head-on. The tiny room, freshly scrubbed as before, brought back that fatal day. Shaky, I peered into the mirror. The red scar on my forehead beamed at me. In a panic, I dabbed on more concealer.

The sedan was gone, the station empty when I went to pay. Inside, Philip stood behind the counter. His eyes twinkled. "Tell me, Emily Johnson, do you like salmon?"

I paused for a moment, not understanding the question. "Salmon?" I said and handed him my credit card. "Yes, I like salmon. Why?"

"Good, because I'd like to ask you to dinner. Our little village restaurant has a great salmon dish special today. I'll be off in an hour. We could have an early dinner before you head out. What do you say?"

"Sure." My face burned bright red. "That sounds great. I saw a cute little bookstore in the village where I can easily kill an hour."

Philip looked at his watch. The digitized numbers glowed 4 p.m. "How 'bout 5:15 p.m.? That will give me a few minutes to clean up."

"Great." I grinned. "Looks like you've upgraded your watch too."

Philip laughed. "Yep, and a few other things. We're now fully automated at the station," he boasted. "No website yet, but my sister is working on it."

Stuffed with new and used books and an assortment of souvenirs and gift items, the quaint bookstore exuded a homey feel. I sauntered over to the wood stove and warmed my hands, enjoying the cozy ambiance. After a few minutes, I wandered along several tempting aisles, each bulging with literary merchandise. I plucked out several best sellers and fanned the pages to take a better look. A woman about thirty years old pushed back a curtain from the stock room and came to the counter. "Hello," she said.

"I love this place," I said as I grinned and put the books on the counter. "I could live here."

The woman gave me a bright smile. "Thanks. I practically do."

"You the owner?"

"Yep." She looked at the titles. "Nice choices. I enjoyed both of these." She slipped a store bookmark inside each book.

"What's your name?"

"Sally." She pointed to the bookmark. "We have a website. You're welcome to log on anytime. We ship too."

"Thanks. I like your little village. How long have you lived here?"

"Forever, it seems. I grew up here. My dad was a logger."

"I see." I stared at her for a moment, certain I'd seen her before. "What else is there to do around here?"

"Not much. I'm a EMT nurse on occasion—when necessary. My brother too."

"That's what it is. I knew there was something familiar about you. I had a bad accident near here about six months ago. You must have helped Philip Estes with the ambulance."

"Yes, I remember. Philip is my brother." Sally gave me a long look. "Very sorry about your mother and friend. Terrible shock."

"It still is. That's why I came up here. I wanted to thank Philip, and now you. You guys saved my life. I wouldn't be alive without your help."

"Glad to have been there. It was a nasty accident. Bad weather."

The door opened and Philip strode in. "Hey! I thought I'd find you here. I guess you guys have met."

"We were just talking about you," Sally said.

"Yeah?" Philip looked at me. "How bad was it? I mean, about me."

I laughed. "Oh, you got rave reviews."

"Come on, Phil. You know I wouldn't tell the bad stuff—at least, not yet." Sally laughed.

"All righty then," Philip said, and ushered me out the door. "Ready for salmon?"

We strolled down the main street for several blocks until we arrived at the restaurant. "Right over here," Philip said and opened the front door. "I reserved a table with the best view."

After tucking my package and purse under the table, I gazed out the large picture window. A heavily forested landscape sloped down into a rich valley where a river wound around the conifer trees. The setting sun cast a warm glow across the land. "What a nice surprise," I said. "I didn't expect this."

Philip smiled. "I'm glad you like it. I wanted to surprise you."

I blushed. "You're making me feel very special, Philip."

"You deserve it."

The waiter bustled over and handed us menus. "I recommend the salmon, our special tonight."

"We'll both have that," Philip said, and winked at me. "Right, Emily?"

"Of course."

We kept our dinner conversation light, neither wanting to delve too deeply into the past. Philip shared several funny village stories, and I divulged a few colorful work episodes. It had been a long time since I had laughed so hard. After our meal, we toured around the town square. Most of the shops were open. Their windows, lit with tiny white lights, gave off a charming, fairy-like glow. I felt oddly calm strolling beside Phillip and slipped my arm through his. A strong familiarity resonated between us, as if we'd known each other for eons.

"Thanks for the lovely meal," I said.

"It's my entire pleasure, Emily Johnson."

A sudden, brisk chill swirled around us, breaking the reverie. I shivered and checked my watch. "It's getting late. I should probably get going or get a hotel room for the night."

"Why don't you stay over? I have the day off tomorrow. We could go hiking. There are some beautiful trails around here. That's our main tourist attraction."

My heart skipped. "Twist my arm."

"That little motel over there is charming, reasonable—and clean." Philip pointed down the block to a small establishment. The sign read *Rest at The Crestin*. "When I first came back to town, I stayed there a few nights," he said. "I can vouch for it."

"Sure. I wouldn't mind that. Hiking sounds good too."

When the morning sun peeked through a crack in the dark shades at 6 a.m., I was awake and drinking my first cup of coffee, excited about the hike. Philip was a seasoned hiker and I felt safe in his hands. Somewhere along the trail, I wanted to confess my rather confused emotions about his heroic act. I knew the conversation wasn't going to be easy.

A few hours later we were climbing a steep, wooded ridge behind the gas station where Philip worked. The trail meandered up a ridge that overlooked the highway and gave us a tremendous view of the valley below. About halfway up, I leaned over to catch my breath, panting from exertion. "I need to stop for a few moments. I'm not in the best of shape yet."

"Oh, sure." Philip handed me a flask of water. "Here, have some. It's still nice and cold."

I gulped down the cool, fresh water. "Where are you taking me?"

"Not too far, a few more miles to the top. There we can see the lake. It's a beauty spot I found years ago. Only the squirrels and birds know about it. Oh, and a mountain lion or two."

Fear sliced through me. "You mean a cougar?"

"Yep. Don't worry. I've only seen a few in all the years I've been climbing up here. They usually roam around at night—night prowlers, hunters."

"I'd rather not see one, if you know what I mean."

Philip raised his eyebrows and nodded. "You ready?"

The next half mile or so the trail rose gradually. We moved into heavily wooded terrain, back out again, and up a steeper ridge where the trail narrowed. My daypack grew heavy, and I lagged behind, silently cursing myself. Did I need that extra hoodie and lip gloss?

Philip called out to me. "Just ahead," he said, waiting for me to catch up. "This is the last steep ridge and then we're there."

I gave him a weak smile. "I'll be glad to see the water."

Around the next bend, Philip stopped short. "Mountain lion scat," he said. "Must have come here early this morning. Looks fresh."

Sweat ran down my back. "Should we go back?"

"Uh, I don't think so. He-she is probably long gone. We're on a human trail. Critters can smell us. They usually stay away. We don't have far to go anyway."

I knew Philip was trying to reassure me, but frankly, I wasn't buying it. I felt uneasy, scared. "What do we do if we see one?"

"Stay calm and stand your ground. If we need to, back away slowly. *Don't run.*"

"You first," I said, and pointed ahead.

When we reached the top of the next ridge, we stood on a grassy mound that looked to the south. The wind picked up, moving the tall grass and wildflowers in rhythmic waves around us. The sun warmed our backs. Gradually, my fear subsided, and I felt at peace. Philip was right, it was a beautiful spot.

He pulled out a space blanket and spread it out. "Have a seat," he said. "I brought a snack for us." He laid out a green apple, some wholewheat crackers and a bag of trail mix. Then he cut into the apple and offered me half.

"Thanks, another surprise," I said and took a bite of the apple.

"Water?" He handed me his flask.

I swallowed a big gulp. "Hmm, lemon. I didn't notice it before."

"Yep, just a little. I find it helps revitalize the innards on a hike."

The warmth of the sun soothed me, and I relaxed. "It's nice here. Thanks for the invitation. An outing is just what the doctor ordered." I blushed and stuttered. "I … I seem to be blushing a lot."

Philip patted my hand. "Don't worry. It's my absolute pleasure to be with you today. You look well, Emily Johnson, especially since the last time I saw you …" He frowned and looked away. " … at the hospital. Gosh, I was worried."

"Me too." Tears came to my eyes. "I felt so alone after Mother and Jack died. I still do." I smiled at him. "*But* not today. Today I feel great."

"It shows." Philip stood up. "Ready to go back down?"

"Not yet. Please sit. There's something I want to tell you. I'm … I'm … well, this is difficult."

Philip sat and reached for my hand. He looked into my eyes. "Go on."

"Well, the fact is …" The words stuck in my throat. "I'm … I'm confused about my feelings toward you. I know this sounds forward, but when I saw you again yesterday, my heart leaped." I turned my head and spoke into the field. "It's like an old memory has come forth. An ancient remembrance of some kind. I can't explain it, but it's there. I feel like we've … we've known each other for a thousand years."

Philip squeezed my hand. "Maybe we have."

"You feel it too?"

Philip nodded. His face turned scarlet. "When I first saw you at the station before the accident, I knew then." He looked down at our entwined hands. "This *does* sound silly."

"No! I felt something then, too, but now—now I know." I took a deep breath. "Somewhere on the timeline we were friends before."

"Maybe even lovers," he said.

My cheeks flushed. "Yes, maybe."

At this point, we heard rustling in the trees. I gasped, "Oh, my God."

Philip motioned to me. "Shh. Be still. Don't move."

Suddenly, a doe popped out of the trees. Behind her scurried a little fawn. The deer and baby ran across the small field into the forest.

"Oh, my gosh," I said. "That scared me."

"Looks like we startled the mom too," Philip said.

"I hope the mountain lion doesn't see them."

"Yeah. Let's pack up."

The trek down took less than thirty minutes. "Whew! That was fast." I pushed my hair back. "I must look a mess."

"Naw. You look great, healthy too. Let's stop and have a bite to eat. There's a quaint little café down the road. Not much to look at but the food is great."

The restaurant buzzed with an early lunch crowd. A cute waitress gave Philip a smile and grabbed a few menus. "Glad to see you again, Phil. You two having lunch today?"

"Yes. Hi, Gail. A window view would be appreciated."

"Sure thing," she said and winked. "Over here."

The café resembled a seasoned, downtrodden diner, but the menu sounded good. "What do you recommend, Philip?"

"Just about anything. Everything is homemade. The burgers are the best. Do you eat meat?"

"Sometimes, mostly not. But I do feel like a hamburger today after all that hiking."

Philip nodded and signaled Gail, who whisked over with pencil in hand. "We'll have two of your delicious hamburgers."

"Good choice. Fries or coleslaw?"

"Coleslaw for me," I said.

"I'll take the fries and an iced tea."

"Make that two iced teas."

"You got it. Your order should be out in about fifteen minutes. We're kinda busy this afternoon. I'll get your teas."

Philip stirred sugar into his tea and gave me a serious look. "I have something to tell you."

I frowned. "Oh?"

"I'd like you to know why a healthy, college-educated man is content working at a gas station in the middle of nowhere."

I put down my spoon. "I did wonder …"

"I don't want to bemoan my situation, but I feel, since you confided in me, you need to know." Philip squirmed in his chair. His eyes wandered out the window for a few moments. "I was in a very bad accident about five years ago. Much like the one you experienced." He bit his lip. "Several people died. One of them was my girlfriend."

"Oh. I'm so sorry."

"I was so broken up about it that I quit my job and moved back home. My sister encouraged me to stay for a while, and well, I did. I've grown comfortable here."

"It's good to have family close. I wish I had that. Mother was my only living relative. I was adopted."

Before we said another word, Gail came over with our order. Philip and I passed each other the condiments and ate in silence for a while. "This is delicious," I said and reached for more ketchup. "Say, Philip, what did you do before the accident? I mean what was your profession?"

"I taught creative writing. I'm a writer by profession. Or at least I was. I stopped after the accident. The words didn't come."

"I don't feel much like working in a crowded office right now either. I've worked for newspapers for a long time. Graphics, but the industry has changed, and I haven't kept up."

"Any ideas about doing something else?"

"Not really. I could design books, I suppose. It's just a matter of learning the software, and there's a market for eBooks now. I could live anywhere and work from home. Lots of people do it."

"Heck, yeah. Where are you based now? I mean, have you moved?"

"Yes and no. I sold Mother's house. The deal just came through and now … now, I can move anywhere. I have forty-five days to vacate."

"Why not come here? Life is simple in this little village."

I laughed. "Are you proposing, Philip?"

"Well, no. Yes, sort of." Philip pushed his plate away. "One thing I learned after the accident is to not waste time.

Run with your heart, say what you mean. Life is too short." Philip grinned. "I think I used every cliché in the book, didn't I?"

"Very tempting, Philip, but I'm still feeling confused about, well, almost everything. I'm not the type to jump in with both feet."

Philip gazed out the window for a few minutes. "You don't have to make a decision now, Emily. But think about it. This place is easy to get used to—and we have internet!"

I laughed. "Thank God!" I laid my crumpled napkin on the table. "That was a super meal, Phil. Can I call you Phil?"

"Of course. All my friends do. Let's get you back to the hotel. I'm sure you're ready to move along."

"Well, yes, at least for now. Will you give me some time to think?"

"As much as you need."

I muddled through the long drive home, barely concentrating on the road. My thoughts were on selling Mother's estate, packing, moving, and Phil—especially Phil. His warm embrace when we parted still whirled around me and occupied the interior of my car, squeezing out nearly everything else. I opened the window to breathe.

Once off the freeway and close to Mother's, I felt a familiar nagging push. Fear ran down my spine. An old adversary tapped my shoulder. For my entire adult life, I'd wrestled with abandonment issues and often sought professional counseling when overwhelmed. Mostly, I backed away from relationships when things got too serious, or in the case of Jack, the relationship ended by tragedy. Who was I kidding? I couldn't even spell the word commitment—is it two ts or one?

I texted Phil.

Home safe. Thanks for everything.

Good to know, and you're welcome, he replied. *Keep in touch. Talk soon?*

I gave his reply an emoji thumbs up.

A few weeks passed without further contact from Phil, and I was glad for the solace. Focused on shutting down Mother's affairs, I had little time to mull over Phil's invitation and what it meant to our fledgling relationship. But his presence remained in the back of my mind.

After one strenuous day, I let down my staunch resolve to focus only on moving, and instantly, my thoughts strayed to Phil. I imagined his soft, kind voice and fantasied about a life together. *What would it be like?* I couldn't help feeling we were meant to be and that we *had been* in love in a past life, a tranquil one with family. We had several children, a fine home—and no tragedy.

As quick as the thought came, my mind snapped shut, and I shoved the notion away. *What was I thinking?* I pushed thoughts of Phil away again and again, until late one night, I saw his transparent image sitting on the edge of the bed, smiling, watching me. Waiting.

I stared at his wavering image and couldn't hold back my desire anymore. "Yes. Come," I whispered. The next instant, I felt his body next to mine and imagined his warmth and gentle caresses until I fell asleep. This encounter led to a series of vivid, late night sexual fantasies. On more than one occasion, our heated, impassioned encounters captivated me. Once, I heard Phil say, "Live, Emily!" as we embraced in a steamy tryst.

His etheric presence felt intoxicating, and each time, I imagined falling into his arms. Lusting for one another, we rolled together naked, caressing, kissing. The fantasies were so real, my body quaked with excitement. My heart nearly imploded. Each time our lovemaking catapulted to orgasm, I couldn't breathe until, unable to separate fantasy from reality, I collapsed, unfulfilled and disappointed.

Our nighttime sexual forays continued until the day Phil texted me.

Coming your way. Will you be available for dinner?

I didn't answer immediately. Ashamed of my fantasies, I ran to the bathroom and coughed into the toilet again and again and spewed out my delusions. "Clearly, you've overreacted," I said to my reflection in the mirror. "Phil will never know unless you tell him." My hands shook as I wiped the drool from my ashen face.

His text beeped again, so I stuffed the phone into my purse, but the faint sound continued. I knew I had to answer, but I held him at bay. Meanwhile, I put Mother's delicate, handblown glass vase into a box and concentrated on wrapping the rest of her knickknacks, forcing myself to think of her need for finery. Her obsession still mystified me. I didn't relish such things.

My cell continued to beep. "Go away," I muttered and taped the box shut. Truthfully, I *wanted* to see Phil, but I was scared. The terrified part of me felt commitment looming. In a cold sweat, I wondered if I could do it—

commit, that is. Wrapped in a cloud of confusion, I pulled the shades and huddled in the dark. Mother's voice rang in my ears. "Don't call him back," she said.

But the pull from Phil was strong. His calm, comforting presence enveloped me. He was so close I could almost touch him. I grabbed the phone and read his text again. "Phil won't hurt me," I said. "He saved my life."

Determined to break away from the past, I opened the shades. Sunlight bleached the darkened room with wide strips of brilliant white. The stark contrast of light and dark brought me a sense of clarity. Of course, *I was the problem.* How stupid I'd been. My mouth went dry. I counted back the years to high school when my sixteen-year-old boyfriend asked for his ring back. I remembered the shock of being in and out of love in less than five minutes. Truth be told, I had not been in love with him—or Jack either. Ours had been a friendship, one of convenience. Still, my heart hurt when he was whisked away.

A renewed sense of grief surrounded me. Heartsick and lonely, I felt unable to grasp a future with Phil. I'd had enough therapy to know I wasn't a schoolgirl anymore. At thirty-five, I was fragile, worn down from the accident and the loss of Mother and Jack. Yet, Phil's gentle, unconditional support gave me hope, and I latched on to it.

Willing myself to believe in a future with Phil, I ignored Mother's warning. Her dislike of men had always colored my upbringing. I'd spent hundreds of dollars in therapy to get over her misguided influence. Still, I sensed her hovering, wanting to protect me. She was my mother after all. Teary-eyed, I sat down and with shaking hands tapped a reply to Phil:

Yes. Please come. When can you get here?

~

"You've been on my mind a lot," Phil said. We were seated in a plush booth at a popular restaurant near the water.

I blushed. "I've been thinking about you too."

Phil reached for my hand and gently squeezed it. "I missed you."

I swallowed hard. "I missed you too." The slight, warm pressure of his hand felt good. I looked into his eyes. "I wanted to see you. Thank you for coming."

"I've arranged a few days off," he said, smiling. "I thought we could spend a little time together if that's all right with you."

"What did you have in mind?"

"I hear there's a great theater in town. My sister suggested the museum and art show too. I … I don't know if you're interested in such things, but she thought you might be."

"It would take my mind off, well, packing … and Mother. Where are you staying?"

"I've got a Airbnb near your mother's house. Again, my sister's idea. She looked it up. Wi-fi is amazing, isn't it? And I was just getting used to the credit card machine." Phil laughed.

"You could help me move a few boxes tomorrow. The movers are coming in the afternoon to take her belongings to storage. She has so much. I don't know what to do with it all, but I have to get out of the house soon. It's been sold."

"Sure. I'd be happy to help. What about finding someone to organize an estate sale for everything you don't want?"

I rolled my eyes. "That would be most of it ..."

"I take it your mother hadn't downsized yet."

"That's putting it mildly. Plus, our tastes are different. She was into fine china, silver, Ethan Allen. I'm not.

"I've pared-down considerably myself." Phil chuckled. "Now, I'm into garage sale's finest."

I smiled and looked down at our hands. "I'm used to living along those lines too."

Phil squeezed my hand again. "I like being with you. I'm interested in spending more time together. What are your plans after ... after you're finished here."

The soft pressure of Phil's hand felt reassuring. My heart fluttered. *What did I want?*

"I ... I don't know. I could do anything, I guess."

"Why not come to Oregon where I live? Oregon has a pleasant livable environment. You could settle there."

"Maybe. It seems a little remote. I don't know if I'd like that or not."

Phil pulled back and stared into my eyes. "You could try it for a few months. No pressure from me. I think you might like the friendly, supportive atmosphere. We could go camping, take a few hikes, enjoy life. Get to know each other better."

"Yes, that would be nice, but what would I do for work? I'd want to work, even with Mother's inheritance."

"My sister might need some help. Uh, part-time, I think she said. It's her idea. You'd have to talk to her for more details."

"I love her store and I am, well, a reader. I design books too. Did I tell you that?"

Phil laughed. "I can see your mind working already. Well, let's just leave it at that. Come on." He picked up the check. "Care for a little stroll before we part?"

I don't know how I managed to have an estate sale, move, and land in Oregon with my belongings in a month's time. After I turned the key to my rental, I walked in and collapsed with a big sigh. Here I was in my new life and, for a few hours I was happy.

I'd kept my arrival date a secret. I wanted to surprise Phil, so when I drove into town, I bypassed the gas station and Sally's bookstore. After a quick shower, I slid into a fresh set of clothes. Filled with joy and giddy with anticipation, I went to the gas station, expecting to see Phil, but the station was dark and the door was locked .The sign on the door said: *Out of town.* I stared at the sign. Phil hadn't mentioned this. I texted him and waited a few minutes. When there was no reply, I drove to the bookstore.

A deep, troubling ache rumbled inside me as I parked in front of Sally's store. It was closed too. A sign on the window read: *Closed due to family emergency. Call 205-665-7834 for more info.* My heart sank. Something was terribly wrong. I stabbed in the number. My stomach dropped when I heard Sally's recorded voice. There had been a fishing accident and a family member—her brother—was missing. Stunned, unable to imagine Phil dead, I went to my rental, lay on the bed, and sobbed in the darkened room for a long time.

The dream was deep. I fell into a dark hole—down, down, down I went. I thought my fall would never end until, as if shot from a cannon, I landed on a green field. The shock unnerved me, and I bolted upright in the moist grass. It was daylight. Ahead, the deserted field stretched as far as I could see. The air, thick with the scent of spring rain, washed over me. "Where the fuck am I?" I said.

"You're here … with me," Phil said. The familiar tenor of Phil's voice startled me. I heard him but I could not see him.

"What happened, Phil? Why are we here?"

"I made a mistake. I'm so sorry. I didn't want this to happen."

"What DID happen?" I rose to my feet and turned around and around. Still, I could not see him. "Where are you? Are you dead? I … I don't understand."

"Just know I love you and I'm terribly sorry our time together was so short."

"I … I came to Oregon to be with you. I wanted to surprise you, and now you're dead?"

"Yes, I am. It was an accident." His voice trailed away. The next moment, I was alone.

"God, I hate this," I said. "I … I don't know what to do. I don't know what to do …"

I woke, still repeating my words. For a moment, I didn't know where I was or what day it was. I checked my watch. Saturday, late afternoon. I'd been knocked out for a day.

At first, I took it for granted that I could somehow—and don't ask me how—talk to Phil, even though he was dead. I held onto the phenomenon as if it was the most natural occurrence. Maybe it is in some cultures but, honestly, I'd never had that kind of experience until Phil died. I didn't know anyone else who had either.

After Phil passed, it wasn't long before I developed what I can only call a dual life: one in the present and the other, well, the other was dream-like—a contrived space I envisioned beyond the ethers where I communed with my dead boyfriend. Some might say this unconscious effort helped me cling onto the memory of Phil. Maybe. I did feel comforted and loved, especially when he came to me in dreamtime, and we reminisced about our past lives together: the love, admiration, joy. These episodes seemed real to me— more vivid than my waking life. I vowed to keep my *affair* with him private. I know enough about psychology that if I confessed to *voices in my head*, I'd be diagnosed with schizophrenic tendencies and be put on medication, if not locked up. So, I made a pact with myself not to tell Margaret, my therapist—no matter what.

Once I was over the shock of Phil's death and my distress abated, the visitations became less frequent. That's when Sally hired me part-time. I loved being there around her energy. She exuded similar vibrations as Phil and her easy presence helped dissolve my sorrow. As the months rolled on, I regained my equilibrium and decided that small town living in Oregon without Phil wasn't for me.

"Oh, gosh," Sally said. "I really enjoy your company and you handle the shop well, but I understand. Really, I do."

"Thanks, Sally. I came here because Phil encouraged me, but now, without him, I feel the need to move on."

"I know what you mean, Emily. He was a comfort to me too. I miss him every day."

"I've made arrangements to leave at the end of the month. I'm sorry." My eyes watered. I pulled out a tissue. "I want to thank you for all your support and kindness. I know this has been a difficult time for you too."

Sally hugged me. "I'll miss you, Emily. Please, please keep in touch. I want that and I know Phil would want that too."

"Of course. I'll stop by before I take off."

The last conversation I had with Phil happened as I drove out of town. In remembrance, I decided to stop by the gas station before leaving. A young attendant hopped out of the office when I drove in. "Yes ma'am, what can I get ya?"

"Fill it up, please."

"Unleaded?"

I smiled, remembering my first encounter with Phil. "Yep, and I know where the restroom is. Thanks."

Clear blue sky and dry pavement signaled a good omen for me as I pulled out of the station. Beneath my calm determination, a ripple of bittersweet emotion wafted through me as I stepped on the gas. It was then I heard Phil's voice.

"Goodbye, Emily Johnson. You be careful now," he said.

Back in Town

*Anything can happen,
you know,
anything at all.*

Back in Town

A loud rapping noise jolted Franklin from his after-noon nap. He rolled off the divan and sat up. The late afternoon sun cast a wide strip of light across the room that led into his freshly painted vestibule. The knocking contin-ued. Franklin felt groggy and disoriented as he hobbled to the door. "Yes, yes. I'm coming," he said. That's when he heard a familiar voice.

"Franklin! Franklin, let me in!"

He unlocked the slick, modern double doors and faced the broad landing where Lola stood, her bright red hair elegantly coiffed. She pulled off a purple velvet glove and held out a manicured hand. Her red nails matched her red lips. "Franklin, I'm back!" she said with a smile.

"Ah, Lola," Franklin sighed. "I've missed you. Where have you been?"

"Away, darling. Far away … to so many places. I can't tell you how exciting and lofty it's been." Lola paused, pulled off her other glove, and gave him a side look. "May I come in?"

"Oh, of course. Sorry." Franklin gestured down the short hall to the sunken living area.

Lola twirled around in the vestibule and waved her long purple gloves. "You've remodeled." She gave him an impish grin. "How quaint it used to be; *now* you've grown modern."

"I wanted a change. What do you think?"

"Oh, yes. It's you—a new you, I guess." Lola turned toward Franklin and touched his cheek. "So good to see you, dearie. I've missed you."

"It's been a while, hasn't it?" Franklin smiled. "Would you like a drink? I've got some wonderful sherry. Thomas and I bought a case of it on our last trip to Spain."

"Would love it." Lola wandered around Franklin's living room for a few minutes while he prepared the drinks. Dense gray clouds swept over the sky, shutting out the sunlight. On the street below, dark shadows lined the cobblestones. "Do you still like it here? I mean in Copenhagen. It seems chilly and a bit dreary, don't you think?"

"Not really. I'm used to it, plus, I get out. Thomas loves to travel, and we take a sunshine break about every six months or so. Living here gives us a chance to go to Spain and Italy. We like Greece and Croatia too."

"Oh, yes. I've been to all those places. Now, I'm interested in the United States. It's my alma mater, as you know."

"Have you seen Charles?"

"God, no. He's such a bear. I can't stand to even think about him."

"He *is* your brother."

Lola frowned. "I know but we've never gotten along—ever."

"Why not make amends and try? You're family and getting older."

Lola walked to the window. She swung around to face Franklin. "I can't, darling. Believe me, he's impossible."

"What's in the U.S.?" Franklin handed her a glass of sherry.

"Money. I'm going on a road trip … to sell my books. It's all arranged. I have a publicist now. Jane. Very nice *and* she's smart! She keeps me on my toes."

"I can't imagine anyone doing that."

"Oh, come now, Franklin." Lola laughed. "You used to."

"In a friendly way, I suppose I did."

"You certainly *did*! Where would I be without you, dear, dear Franklin?" Lola downed her sherry and held out the glass. "Another?" She blushed. "I do love sherry."

"Of course. I hear you have another book out."

"Yes. Jane says it's going to be a bestseller … my magnum opus."

"I enjoyed your last story, a bit sad, though … at the end, don't you think?" Franklin topped off his glass and poured another round for Lola.

"Oh, you're too much of a romantic, Franklin."

"But did he have to die?"

"You can't always have a happy ending, dear. It's just a story for heaven's sake."

"But I love happy endings."

"That's what I mean, most people do—too predictable for me. I like to change it up." Lola stretched her arm out. "Come now, let's go for a walk. I want to show you something. You'll never guess what it is …"

They strolled down the bustling boulevard toward the train station. "Let's hop on the A-train," Lola said. "My apartment's not too far. I'll get the fare." Lola swiped her bus pass and motioned to Franklin. He shadowed her as she weaved through the loading passengers.

Fifteen minutes later, Lola unlocked the door to her apartment. "Now close your eyes, Franklin," she said. " … and stand right here." Lola motioned to the edge of a colorful kilim which covered the entry floor. Lola giggled. "Keep them shut, Franklin. No peeking."

"I am, I am. For heaven's sake, Lola. What's the big secret?"

"Just wait, darling."

Franklin heard a bustling noise.

"Okay. Now open your eyes."

"Oh. My. God. Lola." Franklin gasped. "Another one?"

"Uh-huh." Lola grinned. The chicken squawked. "Franklin, meet Leanora, Henry's cousin."

About the Author

As author, illustrator, and book designer, RA Cook published her first book, a children's picture book entitled *Calvin Splinter & His Splendid Splinter Ideas* on her seventieth birthday in 2018. Inspired by a five-day visit to Iceland, *GIGANTA, An Epic Tale*, a middle grade book highlighting Iceland's legendary trolls and elves, was released in 2021; a limited edition short story entitled *Lola's Muse, A Story of Whimsy and Wonder* came down the pike in 2022.

By early 2024, Cook had published her magical realism novel *Going Out the IN Road*, a thought provoking story about time travel and multidimensons. After a successful launch, she began expansion on a collecton of magical realism stories: *Lola's Muse, A Short Story Collection of Whimsy and Wonder*.

Cook lives with her dog, Stuart, in the Pacific Northwest. She posts her work on Facebook (RA Cook/Becca's Books), Instagram (beccasbooks.calvin), and Substack (Substack@ racook). You can also keep up-to-date on her latest work at www.hmapublishing.com.